Elaine

You think you're so super,
Elaine.

The world's your domain,
Elaine.

What you don't realize,
Little Pretty Blue Eyes,
Is that you're not all that great
With your temper and hate
And you give me a pain,
Elaine.

Books by Stella Pevsner

AND YOU GIVE ME A PAIN, ELAINE
CUTE IS A FOUR-LETTER WORD
LINDSAY, LINDSAY, FLY AWAY HOME
SISTER OF THE QUINTS

Available from ARCHWAY Paperbacks

ME, MY GOAT, AND MY SISTER'S WEDDING

Available from MINSTREL Books

AND YOU GIVE ME A PAIN, ELAINE

Stella Pevsner

AN ARCHWAY PAPERBACK
Published by POCKET BOOKS
New York   London   Toronto   Sydney   Tokyo

An Archway Paperback published by
POCKET BOOKS, a division of Simon & Schuster Inc
1230 Avenue of the Americas, New York, NY 10020

Published by arrangement with The Seabury Press, Inc.
Library of Congress Catalog Card Number: 78-5857

ISBN: 0-671-68838-3

First Pocket Books printing April 1981

17   16   15   14   13   12   11   10   9

*For Mary Shive
and Avery Krashen
and enduring friendships*

1

They were at it again, my mom and Elaine. I could hear them—or rather, my sister—shouting up a storm behind her closed bedroom door as I came into the house.

I tiptoed, although there was no need for it, into my room, threw my books on the bed, and headed for the kitchen. I needed something warm, like milk, to settle my stomach before they came charging out of there.

Warm milk might sound strange as the preferred drink for a thirteen-year-old, but I have a very old stomach. It ties itself into knots during domestic dramas, which are practically daily occurrences, thanks to Elaine. While the stuff heated, I reached for the phone to call Robyn.

I punched out three or four buttons, then heard the door open across the hall and Mom saying, "That's the way it's going to be." The door slammed, and the stereo shot on full blast.

1

I hung up and reached for the pan.

"Did you hear that?" Mom asked, coming into the kitchen. It wasn't a question that called for an answer. "Andrea, your sister is impossible."

I knew that. Everyone knew that. I was curious about the current details, but curious or not, I'd get them anyway.

"The school called again. She cut classes and went roaming off somewhere."

"Why?"

"Why? Because she felt like it. That's exactly what she told me. So now what am I supposed to do?"

The milk wasn't very warm. "Why don't you just leave her alone? It's her problem."

"Sure. That's easy to say. But what if Elaine doesn't graduate next year?"

I felt like saying, "That's her problem too," but at a glance I could see Mom was in no shape to take me on too. "Don't worry. Why don't you go lie down for a while? I'll start dinner."

It scared me, the way Mom was cracking up, bit by bit. From a certain distance, on good days, she still looked young and bouncy, but up close and especially at times like this, you could see the lines inching out from her eyes and the gray sneaking in along her center part.

"Go lie down. That's a good doggie."

My feeble attempt at humor didn't even register.

"I guess I'll go call Rosemary." Mom headed for her room.

If Mom's friend Rosemary charged by the hour as a phone-in substitute shrink she'd be a rich woman today. But I was glad Mom had someone to talk to outside the family. Rosemary always told Mom it was "the age" or something like that.

I still wanted to call Robyn, but the only other line was in Elaine's room, and I wasn't about to enter that snake pit. Besides, she's a stinker about letting anyone else use her personal phone. Elaine is really hot when it comes to her rights.

I noticed chicken on the counter by the sink, thawing. Too much. It still hadn't registered with Mom that both Dad and I, built the same, on the thick side, were trying to cut down. In a way, I think Mom was still cooking for Joe, although he'd been back at college for more than a month now.

A month. It seemed like forever. There was no way I could get used to my brother being away.

I find it almost impossible to describe the special feeling between Joe and me. "The first time I ever saw you," he once told me, "I could have sworn you winked at me. And I knew we'd get along."

We did. Sometimes we talked a lot and sometimes very little, but it seemed as though our thoughts were always in touch.

I'm not saying it was a case of Joe and me against the world. Joe had an easy way of blending into most situations. Things never got too heavy when he was around. "Lulu," he'd say to Mom, "you're really somethin'," and Mom would drop about ten years on the spot. Joe had started the Lulu bit when he was about three, his version of Lucille. He'd been like a baby brother to Mom because she was only eighteen when he was born. And to think Elaine was at present sixteen. It curdled the soul to imagine her as a mother.

Joe and Mom were on a buddy-buddy basis, and Joe and Dad were like adult friends. A year or so ago Joe and Elaine went through a knock-down, drag-out stage, but now they mostly ignored each other. I don't think she even told Joe good-bye when he left for college, gunning his Kawasaki, but I can tell you, when the sound of that motorcycle died out, I felt like falling apart.

"Joe!" I ran water over the chicken, dried it, and arranged it in a baking pan. "Why did you have to go off and leave me with all this?" Pure rhetoric, because I knew full well he had his junior and senior years to finish. "You can't expect me to take your place with Mom. I'm not the cheerful type." It was true. "Miss Moon," they used to call me, when I was little,

4

round-faced, and solemn. Mom didn't know how to take me, after sunny, smiling Joe and Elaine. Elaine, I am told, was a sparkling child, which just goes to show you can never tell about kids.

I picked up the phone, but Mom was still on the line, saying, ". . . how she could be so mean. Rosemary, she acts as though she hates me."

"Hey, Babe, that's just a stage she's going through. You just try to keep your sense of humor and before you know it—"

"Sense of humor! I think I'm losing my mind."

"Why don't you come over to the shop and lose it among friends? I've got these big weddings coming up and . . ."

I eased down the phone, knowing that Mom would reply that she'd love to help out at the florist shop, but she had to stick around and keep an eye on what was going on.

She had good enough reason to say it. Last month when Mom, Dad, and I were at Open House, Elaine's friends swarmed in like a pack of rats and took over the place. They charged off like crazy when we got back, with one of the cars doing a lawn job. Later on Dad found a couple of beer cans, tossed in the front hall closet, and another out by the driveway. "So sue me," Elaine said in that defiant way of hers. "The guys are old enough to drink."

5

After dribbling a mixture of Italian dressing
and honey over the chicken and shoving it into
the oven, I went downstairs to the basement.
Here, in front of the workshop section and the
laundry setup, was my special room. I flicked
on the lights.

None of the kids at school, not even cousin
Katherine (especially cousin Katherine, blight
of my social life), knows about this room and
what I do in it. Don't get the idea that it's some
kind of place where I go to brood. It's, in fact,
exactly opposite. It's where I privately practice
gymnastics.

Gymnastics, as you may know, is required
in eighth grade phys. ed. classes and is loathed
by girls who expect to make it through life
strictly on looks, like Elaine. I didn't want to
appear too eager when our gymnast instructor
first herded us to the balancing beam and didn't
let on that I already knew the maneuvers. Even
so, Miss Tindall said just last week, "Andrea,
for someone your size, you show a great deal
of aptitude." *Someone your size.* Wouldn't that
lead you to believe I'm gargantuan instead of
merely a bit thick in the middle?

Anyway, after class, she took me aside and
asked if I'd ever thought of going into training.

"What do you mean?"

"There's a coach over in Lafayette who
works with girls evenings and on Saturdays.
Bonnie Knudsen, a sophomore who made it to

the state meets, was one of her students. I have a feeling if you'd start working now, by the time you're in high school . . ."

All I could think to say was, "Lafayette's pretty far away."

"Fifteen miles? Couldn't someone drive you?"

"My dad works nights a lot. And Mom's . . . busy." I had no intention of telling Miss Tindall that Mom's busyness meant not only keeping track of my sister but also guarding the house. If word got out that the place was empty it would be up for grabs.

"Why don't you think about it at least?" Miss Tindall looked as though I was just lazy.

I nodded and shuffled off to the showers.

I'd thought about it then, with water streaming over my shoulders, and I thought about it now as I checked out the equipment.

Joe, who's quite an athlete himself, had got Dad to set up this balancing beam for me. With three years of practice I was into some rather complicated moves. But at first, when the beam was still on low, I'd lacked confidence.

"You can do it, Andrea," Joe had said then. "I'm right here. Touch me now and then if you need to." I didn't need to touch him any more, but I needed to have him near. Joe, I thought, pulling off my shoes and getting on the ankle socks, why is it that when you're around I'm somebody special? And when you're away . . .

I was near one end of the beam, poised to do a pirouette turn, when I heard a clattering on the basement stairs. Judging from the noise, it could only be Elaine in those crazy clogs. I did a dismount and readied myself for attack.

My sister came into sight and stopped. She was wearing a new pink crocheted halter that really showed off her chest. Tossing a stream of hair over one bare shoulder, she shouted, "Bug brain, can't you *hear?* I've been yelling myself hoarse."

No big news there. "What do you want?"

"What do *I* want?" Elaine gave me a you're-too-much kind of look. "You have a call. On *my* line."

"Who is it?" I followed her up the stairs.

"How should I know? I'm not your social secretary. Just tell her for me to use the family phone in the future. And if it's busy, *wait*." Elaine cut off to the kitchen, and I went to her room. Elton John was belting it out full blast. I turned him down and picked up the phone.

"Listen," Robyn said, "I've been thinking it over, about the class play, and decided it's just not my *métier*. I'm more for the written word."

"Couldn't you do both? The play's not until next spring, remember."

"I know. But by then, I'll probably be staffing the yearbook as well as doing the 'Ask Iris' column."

"Why 'Iris'?"

"Like the eye. Sees all, knows all. Try to think of a problem, will you, and write a letter, to start the thing off."

That was ironic, because the big problem of my life came flashing back into the room just then, Coke in hand. "Knock it off," she said, turning the music back full volume, "and keep your sweaty little paws off my stereo!"

"Sorry, Robyn, there's a maniac loose in here. I'll call you back." I hung up and gave Elaine a look. "Thanks a *lot*."

"Shove off."

"Great. Now even Robyn knows." I wriggled my fingers into my sock and scratched my ankle.

"Knows what?"

"What a jerk you are."

"Who cares? Shove off."

"A pleasure." With dignity I swept from the room just before the door was slammed after me.

"You're a real charmer, Elaine," I yelled. "You should go enter a contest!"

I stomped off to my room.

DEAR JOE:

I missed you at dinner tonight. Your place looked so empty. Elaine's place looked empty, too. Why? Because she wasn't present. And where was she? In her room. As punishment.

9

The punishment, you understand, wasn't *for* Elaine, but *by* Elaine. She's starving herself to make Mom sorry she yelled at her. I can't understand how things get so screwed up around here, with Elaine goofing off, and then

I wadded up the letter and pitched it into the waste basket.

"Keep in touch, champ," Joe had said that day he left. "Let me know how you're doing." Emphasis on *you*. Joe didn't care to hear the continuing saga of Elaine. "Boring subject," he said once, when I was sounding off. "Choose another topic."

"Aren't you *concerned* about the way she's been acting?"

"Acting's the word, all right. But I'm not her audience and care nix about her performance. Your deal."

We were in his room, playing gin rummy. I shuffled the cards. "Someone has to care."

"Deal me out."

I paused, then realized he was speaking allegorically, if that's the word, and went on dealing.

I arranged my hand but instead of studying the cards, I studied my brother. His looks got to me every time. Brown hair with a hint of rust, and curls. Tanned skin after a summer of delivering orders for Dad and taking weekend trips on the Kawasaki, sometimes with Cassandra. (I didn't want to think about his girl friend, even though she was nicer to me than a sister.) And those blue-blue eyes. Joe's and Elaine's were the same. Blue-blue, as I said, but rimmed with black. The black touch was like an artist's signature on a scarf, Super Class. Elaine has hair the same color as Joe's, too. We have a picture of them in an album where Joe is about six and Elaine three, two curly-heads, holding hands, smiling into the camera.

So. Here I sat, no letter written, no homework started, getting disgusted again. And hungry.

From a psychological standpoint this wasn't the time to cut down on food intake. I could just as well wait until this low mood passed.

I remembered that plate of food in the oven, left there by Mom for Elaine (who had probably gone out anyway), and my stomach rumbled. No point in letting that food sit like a sacrifice to the Goddess of Fury when hunger kept a worthy mortal like myself from concentrating.

I kind of slithered to the kitchen.

Dad had beat me to it.

He looked a little shamefaced as I stood there staring at him. "No use letting it go to waste," he said.

Well, why shouldn't Dad eat? What other consolation did he have in life? I could understand him. We were a lot alike in looks and temperament.

"Why not?" I opened the refrigerator and poked around. There was still more chicken.

"Sit down and join me, Miss Moon," Dad said in a gentle voice.

Miss Moon. Suddenly I lost my appetite.

2

One of my crosses in life is the fact that my cousin Katherine sits directly behind me in study hall. I swear my back is permanently polka-dotted from jabs of her ball point. Like today.

Jab, jab.

"What?" barely turning my head.

"You trying out for the play?"

I hunched my shoulders in a shrug, then leaned so far forward the print in my math book blurred. Why should Kitty care anyway, whether or not I tried to get into the play? I hated the way she was always butting into my life.

I eased back. Kitty punched me out again.

"Can you quit that?" I said over my shoulder.

"Well, are you or aren't you? You know, she's not going to cast relatives, it wouldn't look right, and after all, I—"

The teacher monitor chose that moment to

stand and pin a look on us. I bent over my math. Now I knew I'd go to tryouts—to irritate my cousin, if for no other reason. She had it coming.

Kitty is tall and angular and acts as though she's the only person in the whole world who ever broke an arm during her Wonder Years. She got an excused slip from gymnastics this term because—can you believe this?—she convinced some doctor she had brittle bones. "Personally," I told my parents, "I suspect money passed hands," but Dad said I shouldn't malign the medical profession, it had troubles enough as it was.

I was ready to bolt when the bell rang, not only because of Kitty but because next period was lunch, my best subject.

When I whipped into the cafeteria, I waved to Robyn, holding a place at one of the tables, and went through the line. Lasagna was not my idea of wholesome food for building young bodies, but it wasn't really bad, if you could ignore the disgusting comments being made about it.

"It's all set," Robyn said in a low voice when I joined her. "Miss Griffith said I could be *Iris* and she promised absolute secrecy."

"How come?"

"It *has* to be secret. Kids won't write in if they know who's dishing out the answers."

"I guess not." I had trouble opening my milk

14

carton, and then it ripped and spilled. I went off for napkins.

When I came back, there were kids sitting all around us, and Robyn had them going with some story.

"It's true!" she said, laughing and slapping her palm against the table for emphasis. "My parents actually know this couple. They live out in some swank area where all the men are into jogging by dawn's early light. Then they brag about how many miles they can do, on Saturday nights when they're boozing it up."

"So what?" someone said.

"I'm telling you. This one man—I'll call him Fred—actually loathes exercise. So he hires his chauffeur to jog for him."

"What?"

"The chauffeur stays in the distance, waves, and in the outfit, who's to tell? So old Fred gets his rest and still gets credit for doing those laps, rain or shine."

I was making cracks along with the others when I noticed Mr. Midlar eyeing us from his station in the middle of the room.

Mr. Midlar just happens to be the teacher who is responsible for some of the worst moments I can ever recall in all my years at school. He teaches math, has a mustache and an overbite, and spends most of his time in class trying to reduce girl students to the lowest common denominator. No doubt he picked up some of those macho ideas from the military school where he taught until it went broke. But wouldn't you think, coming to a public school, he'd try to have an open mind?

Of course, I do admit he started at our school under a severe handicap. He had my sister Elaine in class.

If there's any one thing that sets Elaine off, it's the slightest suggestion that she's anything less than two points perfect. Midlar wasn't impressed by her looks, but he was impressed by her ignorance and told her so. That began a battle that raged all year. Elaine won. She passed the course.

"How did you ever do it?" I asked.

"Mike Hirsch, you know, that kid who's a living computer, coached me."

"Why would he?"

Elaine gave me a look from those blue, rimmed eyes, and I knew the answer. Charm.

"Do you think Mr. Midlar has mellowed?" I asked Elaine this fall when I found out I had him for math.

"Even if he has, it's not going to do you any good. Not when he finds out who you are."

She was right. Midlar pounced onto my name the first day, and after finding out I was indeed Elaine's sister, never let up. He pick-pick-picked at me every time I volunteered in class, and then when I gave up, he subtracted points for nonparticipation. On tests he invariably hovered behind my desk, making little sounds from the space between his front teeth that set my own teeth on edge.

He was really eyeing us now in the cafeteria, and I wanted to get Robyn to leave, but everyone was still laughing and carrying on.

Midlar bolted toward our table. "What's going on here?"

Robyn simply paused, looking surprised.

"The cafeteria's no place to exchange your smutty little stories. Now clear out, all of you."

As the kids, without a word, scooted off with their trays Robyn said, "I don't believe this."

"Let's go," I said.

"I have ten minutes more, and I haven't eaten my dessert," Robyn said, coolly looking at Midlar.

I could feel my heart thumping, and I eased away, hoping Robyn would give up and follow.

She didn't, and the upshot of it all was she got sent to the office for defying authority.

Later that afternoon in the hall she told me nothing had come of it. "Is he always like this, or is it one of his bad days?"

"He's always like this, and it's always a bad day."

"Maybe he needs help."

"Go to it, Iris," I said.

Although there had been several announcements over the intercom urging one and all to

17

come to tryouts here in the auditorium, not many kids showed up, and the name of the play itself still remained a mystery.

"If she springs something like Shakespeare on us, I'm leaving."

I knew, without turning around, that the speaker was Wesley Cramer. Wesley is a kid whose voice and body are on *go* while his mind stays on *hold*. He has quite a following because of his size, his good nature, and his large allowance.

"I'll leave with you, Cramer," someone said.

"Yeah, why don't we cut out now?" There was a general shuffling.

"Hold it," Wesley bellowed. *"If,* I said. Otherwise, I'm gonna be in it. A play's no great sweat. Not like being on track."

"Your folks really laying on the pressure, Cramer?"

"I can handle it."

So that was the reason Wesley had shown up with his group. *Get involved in some activity. Any activity.* Lots of parents said it.

And now I asked myself what I was doing here. The real activity I wanted to be in was gymnastics. But I hadn't even mentioned the lessons in Lafayette because Mom was always in such a state. So I guess I'd slid into this as second choice. But looking around at all the girls ready to try out, I knew I didn't stand a chance. The best thing to do was leave. Fast.

I grabbed my books, slid out to the aisle, and came face to face with Mrs. Vidal, the director, who was just coming down the aisle.

"Sorry I'm late," she said, "but I won't keep you long tonight, I promise. Why don't you all move down closer to the front? You boys, and you too, Andrea."

Cousin Katherine turned and whispered something to Sallie Spivak, and they both giggled. I slunk into a seat closer to the stage, but only by a couple of rows.

"I must confess," Mrs. Vidal said, facing us from the front, her arms full of scripts, "that I'm a bit disappointed in the poor turnout of males." Then catching herself, she added, "I mean quantity, not quality, of course." She laughed but no one else did. "However, we'll be holding tryouts for two days"—(was this a sudden inspiration?)—"and I hope when the word gets out about what play we're doing, we'll have boys beating down the doors."

"What play is it?"

"Something you can get your teeth into— literally—almost, Wesley. It's called *Count Dracula*." She showed her own perfect teeth in one of her trademark smiles.

Mrs. Vidal teaches general English to seventh and to top students in eighth. I had her last year. She looks like one of those put-together people you see on TV commercials, enjoying a low-cal drink while draped on a sailboat. She used to get on my nerves at times in class because of her constant enthusiasm. I wondered if she took diet pills.

"I'm sure you've all heard of Dracula," she said now, almost flirtatiously.

"Yeah. He was that ghoul who slept all day and then at night went after people and bit 'em in the neck." So saying, Wesley lunged at the guy next to him and practically knocked him out of his seat. This set off a lot of screeching and jumping around until the place was in an uproar.

With her free hand Mrs. Vidal touched the knotted scarf at her neck. "I realize," she said, raising her voice above the hubbub, "that in choosing a play like this, I could be asking for a lot of cutting up. However"—the kids quieted down some—"I have full confidence that everyone in this auditorium has the maturity to handle it."

This was part of her standard patter. I could imagine Mrs. Vidal saying to a two-year-old child of her own, "I know you have the maturity to look at but not touch Mother's crystal ash tray." Her kid probably would have. The maturity, I mean.

"Tell you what," she said with another of those winning smiles, "why don't I describe the play today, and then tomorrow we can get down to tryouts? Is that agreeable with every-one?"

If someone had said no, she'd have just said "tch," laughed, and gone on anyway. But no one did.

She put the scripts on the edge of the stage, folded her arms, and said, "The play opens in an insane asylum." She paused, smiled at Wesley, and said, "I know what you're going to say. 'Like this school.'" Wesley grunted. "But not quite. There are these English people—I'm not going to ask for accents though—who live out in a deserted area. The only other building within sight is a castle. And in this castle lives Count Dracula . . ."

3

Elaine was almost decent at dinner that night, until she got on the subject of my appetite. I was helping myself to seconds when I noticed her disgusted look.

"Something wrong?"

"If you'd only slim down some."

"I do things for exercise. Not like you, sitting on your buns all day. When you aren't washing your hair."

"It's the way you eat."

"What's wrong with the way I eat?"

"Each meal's like a condemned prisoner's last. You don't eat. You shovel it in."

"That's not true!" (Was it?) "Besides, I'm a growing girl," I said.

"Sure, sideways."

I wasn't all that fat. I wasn't in fact *fat*. I was just a little solid. Someday, if there was any justice on earth—which I was beginning to doubt—Elaine would be all flab with no muscle tone whatsoever and I'd be fit. And slim.

"Leave her alone," Dad said.

Elaine cast a glance at Dad's solid middle, glanced at his face and then away.

Dad put down the roll he'd been about to butter. "Girls, what's new in school?"

Elaine got this tight, hard look on her face and said nothing. She was probably back to attending classes, but she wasn't going to do a Show-and-Tell number about it.

I broke the silence with, "We had tryouts, or at least a meeting, for the class play after school."

"Oh, really? What play?" Mom asked.

"Count Dracula."

Elaine muttered, *"God."*

"And what part have you decided to do?" Dad asked, as though just like that I could have any part I wanted.

"There are only two girls in the whole show, and Katherine's trying out."

"I don't understand," Dad said. Mom looked puzzled too.

I shrugged. "Katherine will be the older woman, and the other one is a sweet little thing who turns into a vampire."

"Hardly your type," Elaine said.

"Andrea can do anything she makes up her mind to do," Dad said. "She has determination." He picked up the roll again and put it

23

down. Poor guy, now he was getting self-conscious.

Elaine couldn't take the slightest little rebuff. "Oh, sure," she said, crumpling up her napkin. "Andy-Dandy has everything going for her. Why not? She's the baby of the family, and everyone caters to her." She pushed back her chair and stalked from the room while Mom and Dad exchanged distressed looks.

I took a few more carrots. "Elaine just wants to get out of doing the dishes. Again."

"She did set the table," Mom said, looking at the door as though something of Elaine remained there.

"Big deal." I finished eating, and then knowing full well Mom wasn't going to put herself in jeopardy by rapping on Elaine's door and telling her to haul her bod out to the kitchen, I started gathering up the dishes.

"Oh, Andy, I forgot. There's a letter for you," Mom said, getting up to help. "From Joe."

"From Joe!" I rushed the dishes out to the kitchen and then tore out to the hall table where we keep our mail.

I picked up his letter and saw what was lying under it. My first six-weeks' grades. No one had opened the envelope, although it was addressed to my parents. I should have been glad, I guess, that they assumed I'd done well, but in another way I felt neglected. Didn't they care?

I took both envelopes to my room and opened the report first. Wow. Borderline. With hard work I'd always managed to squeeze onto the B honor roll, but with these grades, no way. I was disgusted with myself, but I felt a little defensive, too. How could a person concentrate with so much commotion around the house all the time?

"Turn it down!" I yelled at Elaine's wall. There were two closets, hers and mine, between us, but even if it had been open space she couldn't have heard, not with that noise. I went into my closet anyway and banged on the wall. All I got from the pounding was a sore fist.

"Pig."

I flopped onto the bed and opened Joe's letter.

HI CHAMP—
How's it going? Before you know it, we'll all be whooping it up at your graduation! (I promise not to embarrass you by taking flash pictures.)

Andy, would you do me a favor? Try calling Cassandra and ask her what plays. I've tried calling her whenever our hall phone is free, but there's never any answer. She can't be going on that many flights. If you reach her, ask her to call me late, here at the dorm, or else send me her schedule for this month. Appreciate it.

The bike's in for repairs, but when it's fixed and Cassie's around, I'll come home for a weekend.

Love,
JOE

Oh, great. A big fat bunch of stuff about *Cassandra*. I shoved Joe's letter and the school report under my desk blotter and went to the kitchen.

Dad was rinsing dishes, and Mom was putting them into the dishwasher. "I'll do that," I said.

"It's all right, Babe. You really do do more than your share of the work." Mom glanced at Dad.

The phone rang. Robyn.

"How were tryouts?"

I went through the whole spiel again, keeping the Kitty remarks down to a minimum because of Dad. Dad doesn't exactly believe Katherine is the answer to youth-gone-astray, but she *is* family. As part-owner of a sporting goods store, Dad has learned to get along with all types and to take a lot of garbage. He also takes stuff for acid indigestion.

"I'm doing some fake letters just to get rolling," Robyn said. "With luck, my fond readers will pour out their problems from then on, and all I'll have to do is straighten out their lives."

She rambled on, and my folks, finished, left the room.

"I ought to do some studying," I said finally, glancing at the clock. "My grades are murder."

"I know what you mean."

She didn't, of course. Robyn was a brilliant student.

In a few minutes we hung up and I was halfway down the hall to my room when the phone rang again. I got it on the second b-r-ring.

"Now what," I snapped out, knowing Robyn wouldn't take it seriously.

"Hey, is that any way to greet a guy?"

"Joe!"

"Hi, Chuckles. Was that you tying up the line just now?"

"Yeah. Joe, I just read your letter."

"That's why I called. I heard from Cassandra. She's been in the hospital, in traction. Low-back pain. Didn't call before because she didn't want to worry me, she said."

"She okay now?"

"Yeah. She's due out this weekend. I may be home to help her get back to her place."

"You said in your letter that the Kawasaki's in for repairs."

"There are busses running."

27

I felt a twinge. I should have been glad Joe was coming home, but shouldn't it have been for other reasons? Like to see us? Me?

"Hey, Andy, what's the matter? Why the silence?"

"I was just thinking how glad I'll be to see you," I mumbled.

"Same here. How are things going at school?"

I hesitated, but it was better to tell him now, with the toll charges clicking away. "Not too well. My grades stink." And then before he could comment, "Joe, listen, it's not easy to study these days. You wouldn't believe the way Elaine has been carrying on around here."

"So what else is new? And what has that to do with you?"

"I just can't concentrate."

"Come on now! Don't give me that!"

"Well . . ."

"If you're going to start handing out alibis, Andrea, forget it. I don't have time to listen."

"Joe, come on—oh, all right. Maybe I haven't put in the effort. But honestly, Joe, it isn't easy."

"Easy is something else."

"Okay, I get it. Want to talk to Mom or Dad?"

"Just tell them I'll be home. So long, Andrea."

I went to my room and did try to concentrate. Suddenly I realized an hour and a half had slid by. I'd done it! But then I realized the sounds had silenced in the next room. Elaine must have gone out.

To ease the strain of all that study, I decided to take a long, warm bath.

Lounging in the tub, lifting up layers of bubbles on my legs, my thoughts drifted to Cassie. Joe had met her a year ago this past summer when he flew to New York to visit some friends. She and another stewardess lived in our suburb because we're near the airport. Then the roommate got transferred to the West Coast. Now Cassandra lives alone. That makes it pretty convenient for Joe when he's around.

I leaned forward to turn on the hot water tap.

Cassandra, Cassandra. Even the name is bewitching. I know she's completely charmed my brother. Since he met her, there's no other girl. It gets to me sometimes when I catch him looking at her, as though he can't get over the wonder of her. Cassie's pretty, in a natural kind of way, and small, and lively. She's older than my brother, but that doesn't seem to matter to him or to the family. Everyone likes having her around. But why does she have to have such a hold on my brother?

I turned off the faucet with my toes and leaned back. The porcelain felt cold on my shoulders.

If I were seriously sick, Cassandra would send flowers or a Candy-Gram, or if she were in town she'd stop by to see me. If I were any kind of a decent human being, I'd haul myself out of the tub right now and go give her a call.

Instead, I let the water grow cool, then added hot, and so on until my fingers and toes wrinkled.

Cousin Kitty makes me sick. Elaine makes me mad. Those are perfectly normal reactions. But why should I feel this resentment toward Cassie, who's never been anything but nice to me?

Why? Because, I guess, I'm not a decent human being.

4

When Cousin Katherine got up at tryouts and read the role of the aunt with an English accent straight out of *Monty Python* I felt like crawling away from the audience on my hands and knees. She did get the part, though, by default, because all the other girls wanted to be the sweet young thing who gets it in the neck.

I probably wouldn't have shown up at the tryouts if Mrs. Vidal hadn't stopped me in the hall during the day.

"Andrea, I've been wondering. Are you interested only in acting, or would you consider being on the technical crew?"

"Uh—technical?" I mumbled, confused.

"You would? Oh, that's super! I've been a bit worried because some of the special effects of this play are tricky, so I'd like someone I can really depend on to be in charge." She gave me the eye-blink-and-smile number, said she'd see me at rehearsal, and took off, her skirt flapping around her legs.

I stood there blinking myself, wondering exactly what it was I'd agreed to do. But at least, I decided, finally drifting down the hall, it wouldn't be as rough or as embarrassing as actually being up there on stage in front of the world.

Getting back to the casting, Wesley got the part of main shrink in the sanitarium. Like all the other guys who tried out (Mrs. Vidal must have spent the whole day collaring kids in the hall), he wanted the part of Count Dracula, but there was no way he could be gaunt. As for sinister—everyone, including Mrs. Vidal, broke up when he read the line, "I cannot dine with you." And, baring his teeth, "I will feast later."

"Yeah, Cramer," someone called out. "At McDonald's."

A kid I knew from science class, John Kossack, had not only the lean, dark, caved-in-cheek look but also a voice that caused shivers when he read the same line, leering at the girl victim's neck. So he was Dracula. The other parts were parceled out, and the players all got scripts.

"Now I need some superdedicated people to volunteer for crews," Miss Vidal said, with her flash-on smile. "In this play the people working backstage are at least as important as the actors. Chris, sitting by himself over there"—she gave Chris Walker one of her flirtatious smiles—"is going to be our lighting genius. We need costume, set, and prop people, and others to help our special effects chairman. The play calls for furniture that moves by itself, screams, dogs howling—" Naturally, this started a chorus of howls. Mrs. Vidal laughed and held up her hand. "Such talent. And there will also be various magic acts."

"Like what?"

"Well, in one scene Count Dracula disappears, and the two men are left holding his empty cape."

"How do you do that?"

She beamed. "Sign up and find out."

Several kids did. I didn't know whether I was supposed to sign up or not, so I just sat there. When the kids were getting ready to leave, Mrs. Vidal called me over and gave me a script.

"As you read it, Andrea, mark the special effects. In the back of the book you'll find explanations of how to do them. Now don't get discouraged," she said, putting a hand on my shoulder. "I'll see that you get plenty of help."

If I'd realized then what I'd let myself in for, I'd have been plenty discouraged.

Miss Star-Is-Born came over and butted right in with, "Mrs. Vidal, how soon do we need to know our lines?"

33

"Don't worry about lines yet, Katherine. First we're going to develop mood and interpretation. Just read the play so you'll get the idea of the character. You're the comic relief, you know."

My cousin looked confused, which is not unusual.

I called home to remind Mom I wouldn't be there for dinner and then trudged out to Robyn's.

"What happened?"

"Nothing much. She just chose the cast. I'll tell you about it. Your parents home?"

"No. We can start the pizza."

We went out to the kitchen, which looked shiny and unused. They'd only lived in the town house since August. Robyn's parents were in the city all day because they ran some kind of photo studio.

"Don't you ever get lonesome?" I asked, as Robyn flicked on the oven switch.

"I'm used to being alone."

"But at least in the city you were near to people."

"Not many kids, though. Not in our high rise." Robyn got out the frozen pizza and pulled off the wrappings. "Besides, it was my choice. I wanted to see what it was like to live in a suburb."

"Big whip."

"Listen, I like it. And it'll be even better in

high school with so much going on. Want to read the sample *Iris* letters I wrote, while the oven's heating?"

We went up a little curved stairway to Robyn's loft room. It was done in beige and brown with coral accents. The desk was against a wide window that looked out toward the manmade lake. Along one wall was a series of plexiglass-framed photographs. The one I liked best was of Robyn at the age of about eight, sitting on a swing. She'd been a model for a while, but even though her parents had an in they didn't push it. "Boring," Robyn had told me. "No strain on the brain."

"Here they are," she said, pulling a sheet of paper from her beige typewriter. "Remember, these are just teasers, to get the kids started writing. I'll be back."

She left. I kicked off my shoes and flopped onto the bed.

DEAR IRIS:
Whenever my dad wants me to do something I don't want to do he says, "It's for your own good." How can I get him to stop?

TEED OFF

DEAR TEED:
That's the way parents are. Don't fight it. I'm telling you this for your own good.

35

DEAR IRIS:
I like this boy but he doesn't know I'm alive.
What shall I do?

PERPLEXED

DEAR PERPLEXED:
Stop playing dead.

DEAR IRIS:
My mother is always hassling me about dump-
ing clothes and food around my room. Yes-
terday she had a fit when she found a dried-up
sandwich in my dresser drawer. I can't take
much more of her yelling. Should I run away?
SICK OF BEING HASSLED

DEAR SICK:
Stick around. Your mother's the one who
should run away.

"You don't like them," Robyn said.

I swung my head around, wondering how
long she'd been standing there in the doorway
looking at me. "Sure, I do."

"But you're not truly moved."

"Robyn, I'm paralyzed. I'm all broken up."
I slapped my palm against my heart. "I'm dev-
astated."

"You should have tried out for the play."

"What I really think," I said, scrunching into
my shoes, "is that the letters you get from kids
will be dull by comparison."

"Then you write one."

"Me? I don't have any problems." I thought, all I have is a wacko sister, a brother who no longer loves me best of all, a mother who takes me for granted, and a father who's headed for an ulcer. Not to mention slipping grades. "How are kids supposed to get to you anyway, Iris, seeing you're such a mystery?"

"There'll be a box in the library. Miss Griffith will be the go-between. And don't ever call me Iris."

As we went downstairs the phone started ringing. Robyn rushed ahead and grabbed it. "Oh, hi. Sure, everything's okay. Andrea's here, and we're about to eat pizza." Pause. "After all that I hope they turn out." Pause. "Sure, I will. See you." She hung up.

"They're developing some food shots."

Robyn told me about the studio and how her parents had all these little special areas for different kinds of shots and how she'd take me in some Saturday, and I told her about the tryouts. By the time we'd finished eating and cleaning up the kitchen it was getting dark.

"I ought to head for home."

"Stick around. We can study together."

"Okay, but I'll have to call to be sure someone can pick me up later."

Mom answered on the first ring. "Oh, it's you," she said.

"What's the matter?"

"I'm just going crazy, that's all. Your sister—"

"Is it all right if I stay here at Robyn's? Can someone pick me up at nine?"

"You'd better come home right away. I don't know what will be happening at nine."

"What's going on?"

"Just come home."

I heaved a big sigh and hung up. "I have to go home because of that creepy Elaine."

"What's the matter with E.?"

"Who knows? Who cares." I got my stuff. "Maybe I will write a letter to Iris," I said.

The late October chill in the air didn't cool me down as I stalked the dreary mile home. It was bad enough that the place was always in an uproar. Why did I have to be part of it?

Mom rushed to the door as I came in. "Oh, it's you," she said.

I was getting kind of tired of those words. "I do live here," I said. "Or hadn't you noticed?"

"Have you heard from Elaine?"

"Mom, I was at *Robyn's*. Where *is* Elaine?"

"That's what we don't know."

"It's early."

"But when she ran out she said she was never coming back."

"She's said that before."

"I think she meant it this time."

"Mom." I put down my books and led my mother to a chair in the living room. I perched on the arm and leaned my head down to hers. "You know the way she is."

"Sometimes I think she's crazy. But she knows very well what she's doing. I'm the one who's losing her mind. Why does she do this to me?"

"Where's Dad?" I guess I'm a very shallow person, because half of my mind was on the conversation but the other half was thinking, I wish Mom would take care of her looks and her clothes the way she used to before she began making a career out of worrying about Elaine.

"Your dad," Mom said, answering my question, "is with someone there at the shop and says he can't get away just now."

"Oh." I gave her cheek a pat and got up. "Have you eaten?"

"Eaten? Andy, I'm going crazy, and you talk about food. It's just sitting out there on the stove."

"How long ago did Elaine take off?" I brushed some newspapers off a chair and slouched down.

"It seems like hours. I've called every friend of hers I can think of, but no one has seen her."

"Or else they're lying."

Mom perked up a little. "You think so?"

"Why not? They always do." I sniffed. "Something's burning out there."

"Burning?" Mom went out, and I picked up my books and went to my room.

Instead of making the most of the quiet, I found I couldn't settle down. It wasn't normal to be in my room and not see the closet doors shake on their hinges.

Finally I got at the books. I heard Dad's car coming into the drive and all the little sounds, the slam, the footsteps, door opening, and then the voices. Next I heard kitchen sounds.

I went out. Mom was scrubbing out a skillet at the sink, and Dad was sitting at the table.

"Here's my girl! Sit down, honey." Dad looked more tired than worried. Both of my parents seemed to be aging before my eyes.

"What are we going to do, George?" Mom asked, still scrubbing away. "It's after nine."

"Nothing. What can we do, call the police and say our sixteen-year-old isn't home yet? At nine? They'd think we were nuts."

Mom ran rinse water over the skillet. Anxiety made her superefficient. When she was relaxed, she drifted around the house talking to things. Really. Like one day a can of peaches fell off a shelf from the cupboard, and when Mom put it back, it fell out again. "Okay," she said. "You can sit out here, but don't think I'm going to open you." It was funny the way Mom

40

did that, but it wasn't a thing you wanted her to do around your friends.

Dad did a few shoulder-lifting tension relievers. "Anything new in your life, Andy?"

"Not much. I'm in charge of special effects for the class play next spring."

"They've started already?"

"Maybe if you drove around," Mom said.

"What?" Dad put an elbow on the chair back and turned.

"Maybe you'd . . . see her somewhere."

"Lucille. Now, you know . . ."

The front doorbell rang.

"Oh, God, something's happened," Mom said.

Dad got up. "Lucille, take it easy."

The girl at the door looked startled when she saw all three of us in the doorway. She backed up a little. "Uh. Hi." She glanced around at some guy in a plaid jacket. "I'm, uh, Sharon."

"Won't you come in, Sharon, and . . ." Dad glanced at the guy.

"No, really." The girl's look skimmed over us and away, and then back to Dad. "I don't suppose Elaine's back yet."

"No, she's not."

"Yeah. Well, I probably shouldn't tell you this, but we saw her a little while ago."

"Where?" Mom pushed forward.

Seeing Mom did something to the girl. She chewed on her lip and then burst out, "Heading

41

north on Route 18. She was trying to get a hitch. We turned around and offered to bring her back, but she said no. It's none of our business, but Elaine's a good kid and—"

"Did she say where she was going?" Dad asked.

"No, but she'd have to be headed for the grove."

"The grove?"

"That's where they deal in drugs," I said.

"What?" Dad whirled around. "How do you know?"

"Everyone knows that."

"Is the grove open this time of night?" Dad asked, turning back to the girl.

"Not really. But there are ways for . . ." she glanced at me.

"I really appreciate your telling us," Dad said.

"Yeah, well, I wish you wouldn't tell Elaine. If—I mean—when she gets back."

At the word "if" Mom looked as though she'd been hit. When she caught her breath, she grabbed Dad's sleeve and said, "George, what shall we do? Call the police—or—?" She looked wildly around toward the kids, but they'd already backed off and faded into the night.

"Thanks," Dad called out automatically as the car screeched away. He put his hand over

Mom's where she was clutching his arm. "Try to keep calm, Lucille."

"Calm!"

"I'll drive out and try to find her before she gets—"

"Gets *what?*"

I felt a little sick inside.

"Before she gets to the grove," Dad said. "Once inside that place . . ."

"First, call the police. Have them help look. No, you'd better leave," Mom said. "Get going. I'll call the police."

As I heard her rushing off I glanced toward the front window and saw a car turn into our drive. Even without the whirling lights or siren I knew what it was. "Neither of you needs to call," I shouted. "The police are here."

"Something's happened!" Mom shrieked.

"No, it hasn't. Elaine's with them." I watched my sister slam out of the lit-up interior of the car, with a cop following right behind her.

Elaine stalked into the house, eyes blazing, and stood stiffly while Mom fell all over her, crying and carrying on.

Dad walked over to the door by the cop, and I could hear words like "hitchhiking" and "ordinance."

Elaine broke loose from Mom and tried to leave for her room, but I blocked the way. "Boy, you really did it this time," I said. "You ought to be shot."

43

I didn't mean it, of course, but wow—the look on Mom's face!

"Andrea," she said in horror. "How can you say something like that, after what I've just been through!"

"I didn't put you through anything. She did. Your precious Elaine!"

"Just cram it," Elaine said, supposedly to me but actually, I thought, to both of us.

"You think you're so grown up," I said to her. "Well, you're not. You're still a spoiled little brat who doesn't care who she hurts just so long as—"

"That's enough!" Mom said. "Go to your room, Andrea. Your father and I can handle this without your help."

"What's going on?" Dad asked, coming over. I heard the car taking off outside.

"Andrea's upset," Mom said.

"Aren't we all. Just a minute there, young lady," Dad said as Elaine started off again. "Not so fast. We have some talking to do."

"Oh!" Elaine looked upward with her famous martyred expression. She flung herself into the nearest chair and, with arms folded, stared straight ahead, teeth clenched. "I've had all the lectures I need for one night from the cops."

"You're lucky you got off so easily," Dad said. "In more ways than one."

I was pretty sure he was going to start in

44

about drugs, thanks to that little crack I'd made about the grove. Actually, I hadn't meant Elaine had gone there to do any dealing. She'd told me herself, some months ago, that she was off the stuff forever, it messed up your head. But I wasn't going to butt in now and help her out. Let her come up with her own story and try to make it stick, as they say on TV.

"All right," Dad said, stationing himself in front of Elaine's chair. "What exactly were you up to tonight?"

"I was *mere-ly* going out to try to find some friends and deliver a message." Elaine folded her arms even tighter.

"A message? What kind of message?"

"That some guys are taking off and will get in touch with these other guys later."

Mom dropped into another chair and leaned toward Elaine. "I don't understand."

"And neither do I," Dad said. "Why you had to go off in the middle of the night and—"

"Middle of the night!" Elaine shrieked. "It's not even nine."

"It's closer to ten," I said.

Mom swung around to look at me. "Go to bed, Andrea."

"Why do *you* have to deliver messages?" I said, glaring at my sister. "Don't your friends know about Western Union?"

45

"Will you two make her get out of here?" Elaine screamed.

"Andrea!" Mom meant business that time.

"Andrea . . . honey . . ." Dad said. "Let us handle this, will you?" He looked so tired. "Goodnight, honey."

"Goodnight," I mumbled. I left, but as I paused in the hall, I could hear Dad say, "She does have a point. Why did you take it upon yourself to go out there all alone?"

"Risking your life," Mom said.

"All right, all right!" Elaine yelled. "So I made a mistake. I should have told you I was going!"

"We'd never have let you," Dad said.

"See? And then you wonder why I do things on my own. "

"Elaine," Dad said, "don't you know what we're trying to say?"

"You've said it a dozen times already! What do you want me to do? Crawl on my hands and knees down Main Street?"

We didn't have any Main Street in our town.

"I'm only trying to make it clear," Dad began. His voice was getting weary.

I went on to my room and closed the door. I didn't need to hear any more. From now on it was going to be the standard stuff, with Elaine picking up any little remark like Dad's *"middle of the night"* to sidetrack them off the main subject. She was a pro in that department.

46

Finally after a lot of high drama she'd end up sniffling and saying she was miserable and misunderstood, but she'd work it all out if people would just leave her alone. Mom would believe it because she wanted to, and Dad would let it go because he could only take so much after a full day's work.

I barged around in my room for quite a while, then finally got undressed, turned off the lights, and opened the door a crack.

". . . worry us like that again," Mom was saying in a pleading voice. I couldn't catch Elaine's answer. I did hear Dad out in the kitchen. He was probably breaking out a fresh jar of that antacid stuff he takes for his stomach.

5

"And they didn't even ground her or anything," I told Joe, that Saturday. We had just dropped Mom off at the florist, where she was going to help Rosemary with a wedding order. Rosemary gave Joe some burnt-orange mums to take to Cassie, and the spicy smell was almost knocking me out. "Elaine gets by with murder."

"Look, chum, why don't you butt out? The folks have their own way of handling it."

"Sure. Hands off handling. It's not fair."

"Who says life is fair? You just do the best you can."

"But they don't do anything!"

"Andrea, kids don't come with directions like appliances. The best parents can do is push different buttons and hope everything comes out all right."

"Good luck."

"Besides, there may be some things you don't know."

"Like what?"

Joe swore softly as a truck hauling road markers came to a dead halt in front of us and turned on yellow blinkers. He threw the VW into reverse and pulled around the truck. "Like Elaine's upset about this Steve guy she's hot on, taking off for Arizona."

"Oh? When did this happen?"

"Lately. Look at that. They've had this road blocked off for months, and it's still not finished."

We eased along the one lane that was open.

"I don't see what Steve's leaving has to do with Elaine hitching out to the grove."

"Her way of getting back, I guess. Doing something dangerous."

"That's not what she told the folks."

"Well, naturally not." Joe came to a halt behind a station wagon.

"Do you think Elaine has shallow roots?"

Joe shifted gears and settled a look on me. "You know, Andrea, sometimes I don't get the way your mind works."

"I was thinking about last summer. When you told Mom not to turn on the lawn sprinkler."

Joe shifted again. "What has water conservation—?"

"Not that. It's what you said. That if you

leave grass alone, it'll dig down to find its own moisture and build stronger roots."

"Yeh, I sort of remember." Joe shot ahead in a sudden cleared space.

"So I was thinking. Elaine has all this attention showered on her. Maybe if everyone would stop trying to protect her . . ."

"She'd have to dig down and survive on her own?"

"Something like that—hey, shouldn't you slow down a little? That sign said we're in the hospital zone."

"It's an emergency," Joe said, swerving into the lot.

"Sure. You haven't seen her for . . . how long?"

"Quiet," Joe said. "And don't attract attention when we get inside. Kids under fourteen aren't even supposed to be in the hospital."

We got out of the car and went into the building. Joe whipped right past the reception desk, where people were milling around, and headed for the elevator. When we got off on the fourth floor, he steered me past a center place where nurses were talking and down a corridor marked 400–432. I got an uneasy feeling from being in a place where I didn't belong and from being stared at by patients propped in beds.

Joe pushed me into a room.

A woman in the first bed glanced at us and then looked back at the TV high on the wall.

In the next bed Cassie gasped and gave a little cry. "Joe! Andrea!"

Joe rushed over then, and I guess kissed her. I pretended interest in the TV, although it was only a commercial for a stopped-up drain.

"Andrea! How nice of you to come see me!" That was my cue to go over, and I got kissed too. "And flowers!"

"Freebies," Joe said. "But the thought's there. How are you?"

"Perfect."

"I know that. But how do you feel?"

Cassie made a little mock smile that produced dimples. "I feel great and I'm about to be released, as soon as my doctor shows and says the magic word."

"Hey. Then maybe we can take you home."

"Three on a bike? I don't think I feel that great."

While Joe explained about coming home on the bus and our having the VW and all, I strolled over and put the flowers in the stainless steel sink and ran a little water over the stems. I could feel the TV woman eyeing me. What if she buzzed for the nurse and had me thrown out?

"If you want to take me home, Joe," I said, going back to the bed, "you could come back and wait for Cassandra."

"Oh, don't rush off." Cassie took my hand. "What have you been doing lately? I've missed seeing you." Her voice had a husky quality which always came as a surprise, considering her delicate looks. "Tell me." She gave my hand a playful little shake.

I couldn't think of anything, so I smiled like a simp and shrugged my shoulders.

"Andy's shy," Joe said. "A backward child. We're thinking of putting her away."

"Oh, be quiet." She gave his hand a playful tap and then began telling us about how she'd been in traction and had everything stretched.

Standing there, still holding Cassie's hand, I thought of how nice it would be if she were my sister instead of—no—in *addition* to . . . But would she change if she married Joe? Was she being nice to me because I was part of the package? I eased my hand away and made little pleats in the sheet. It might even be worse if they married because then Joe would have someone else all the time.

Joe and I hung around until Cassie got her release. I carried her little airline bag and the mums out to the car, and Joe carried some plant and supported Cassie as she shuffled along.

"Andy," Joe said, when we got settled in the car, "why don't I just drop you off at the florist shop?"

"Why?"

"Because it's on the way. I can pick you and Mom up later."

I *was* in the way.

Rosemary, at least, seemed delighted to see me. "Oh, sweetie, can I ever use an extra pair of hands!"

"For what?"

"Your mom's answering the phone, taking orders, and trying to wait on customers." Rosemary pushed up the sleeves of her rust-colored turtleneck top. "I've got the bride's bouquet done and the boutonnieres, but I've just started on the nosegays. Could you help me strip?"

"What?"

"The leaves. Come on, I'll show you."

We went into the back room, which was like a nightmare garden, with buckets full of flowers and greenery sitting everywhere and a work-bench cluttered with wires, tools, ribbons, and clumps of flowers.

"Arlene called in sick this morning, that's why I'm so far behind. You sit there," she pointed to a stool, "and drag off the leaves, and then stick a wire into the stem. Like this. Then I'll wrap them with this tape and get 'em together."

I took one of the button mums and ran my fingers down the stem. The leaves were soggy from having sat in the water and it was pretty yucky, all that greenish goo. I flicked it into the big plastic-lined garbage can.

I took a piece of wire and forced it through the stem. "Ick."

53

"What's the matter?"

"It seems so—kind of against nature to do this to flowers."

"It's a living."

"Not to them. It's sudden death." I watched her start winding on tape and picked up another mum.

"Maybe sudden death is best for flowers when they're in full bloom and before they fade. At least these are going to have their big moment, all fancied up with ribbons and things."

I stripped off more leaves. They clung to my fingers until I rubbed them along the rim of the garbage pail. "If I ever get married—which I seriously doubt—I'm going to carry a bouquet of flowers just as they've been picked."

"That's right, kid. Put me out of business." She flashed a smile and kept on twirling the tape around the stem. "Don't tell me you're a throwback to those flower children of the sixties."

"I'm not much of anything."

"Come on, now."

I hadn't meant to sound so self-pitying. "What I mean is, I don't know what I'm really like. And I don't know where I'm going, or what I can do."

"What's the big rush? What are you now, fourteen?"

"Thirteen."

"Wow! You've just begun. There's plenty of time."

"But they're putting on all this pressure at school. They have career days, with people coming in to tell us about different professions." I stripped another stem and put it on the pile. "And I still don't know."

"They're just presenting some options. That doesn't mean you have to decide."

"But I don't want to drift on and on and be like . . . Elaine."

"Elaine! Are you kidding? You couldn't be like that sister of yours if you tried."

"I guess Mom's told you about the way she's been acting." (Of course, I knew for a fact it went on all the time.)

"Sure, she talks and I listen, but I can't come up with any answers. What can you do, except hope that Elaine snaps out of it? It's a shame. She used to be such a winner of a kid. Always smiling."

"So I hear, but for a long time now it's been Scowl City. "

Rosemary gathered a group of stiffened flowers and wired them together. "Elaine must have her reasons. Could be she's under some kind of pressure or influence. Friends, maybe."

"Friends! You should see those creeps she runs with."

Rosemary slipped the bunch of flowers through a hole in the center of a white doily, and held it out. "If you'll wipe off your hands and hold this for me, I'll tie on the ribbon streamers and we'll be in business. It's lucky for me you dropped by."

I was glad, too, because being around Rosemary always gave me a lift. Although she was the same age as my mother—in fact, they'd been classmates—she always chatted away as though we were old buddies. Mom never talked about having been Homecoming Queen (I guess she thought Elaine wouldn't like it), but Rosemary told me about how pretty Mom had been and how popular. "But kind of shy, too. She liked writing love poems." Rosemary had been more of an extrovert, into school politics, the debate team, and drama.

"Say, Rosemary," I said, "did you ever hear of a play called *Count Dracula?*"

Rosemary eyed the green and orchid streamers and snipped off the ends at an angle. "Sure, I've heard of it. Why?"

"Our class is going to do it."

"No kidding. You in the cast?"

"No. I'm in charge of special effects, like flying bats and chairs that move by themselves."

"I'd like to see that. Let me know when."

We started on the next nosegay. "Did you ever hear of a flower called batswort?" I asked.

"Bats—what?"

"Batswort. It's something they use in the

play to keep Dracula away from the girl victim. See, he can't stand the smell of batswort. The prop people will have to locate some, and I thought you might have it."

"In plays, baby, you improvise. I've got artificial stuff around here you can have. You never use live flowers on stage anyway."

"Why not?"

"It's considered bad luck. Like—oh, step on a crack, break your mother's back. Hey, speaking of backs, how's Joe's girl friend?"

"Fine. He took her home just now."

"The two of them are still going strong, huh?"

"Sure. Why not?"

"I don't know. It seems a strange match. Joe still in college, Cassie off on a flying career. And the age difference."

"Joe doesn't seem to think that's important."

Rosemary shrugged. "Maybe it's not." She twirled away at the stems. "Listen, I'm not out to knock romance. Not when it leads to weddings with lots of flowers."

She looked at me and winked. My face must have betrayed my feelings.

"Hey, Andy, I was just speaking in general. I didn't mean Joe. He wouldn't do anything crazy. You know that."

I nodded. But my brother *was* crazy about Cassie.

6

I've never been much for Thanksgiving. Partly because I have this built-in duty thing that absolutely compels me, the night before the big event, to run over the things in my mind for which I should be thankful.

So I lay in bed thinking, I have both my parents, and while neither is in what you'd call peak condition, they're functioning, and not, so far as I know, thinking of getting a divorce. I'm healthy, I thought. Am I ever. And unless I spend more time working out and less time feeding my face, I'll be a chubby little elf come Christmas. School. Take a skip on that one. I was thankful Joe was home and that he and Cassie would be with us for Thanksgiving dinner. What I wasn't thankful for was that Aunt Ellie, Uncle Herman, and Cousin Katherine would also be with us.

When I staggered out to the kitchen the next morning I heard Mom talking. She was holding this one-way conversation with the turkey which had obstinately refused to defrost itself completely during the night.

"Come on now," she said, running water over it in the sink, "I haven't got all day."

"When do we eat?" I asked, shaking various boxes of cereal. There were about a dozen, most of them nearly empty.

"Oh, Andrea. I'm glad you're up. I'm glad someone's up. I need help. Hardly anything's started, and they'll be here at three."

"What shall I do?"

"Scrub the potatoes. And could you make the cranberry salad? Oh, baloney." She snatched some paper towels off the roller and wiped the edge of the sink where she'd sloshed water. "Maybe, on the other hand, you could set the table. But first, make the centerpiece out of those flowers— Oh, no!"

"What?"

"I forgot the flowers." She stared at me like a little girl who was about to be punished.

"We could use that old wicker horn of plenty if you have any fruit to stuff into it."

Mom whipped over to the refrigerator, water dripping from her hands, and looked inside. "Plenty of fruit."

"Where is it? The horn?"

"Probably in the back closet, with the Christmas ornaments and all that junk. One of these days . . ."

"Maybe Elaine could go find it while I—"

"Elaine?"

"You know. Elaine. She lives here. Sort of."

"Andrea, don't start stirring up trouble. What I don't need is your sister grumping around."

Great, I thought. I get to be the handy helper and Her Highness gets to sleep. Probably dragged in way after curfew. As per usual. "Where's Joe?"

"He and your dad went over to the shop to pick out a heavy leather jacket for biking. But in my opinion it's getting too cold for Joe to ride that Kawasaki anyway. I wish he'd get rid of it altogether."

I set the table first, and then went to the closet to try to unearth the horn of plenty. It looked like *Mission Impossible*. Mom's a saver of all things significant, but she has no sense of order. I found the Christmas decorations and a box of Elaine's and my old ballet costumes, and Easter baskets and outgrown ice skates and even a box of things we'd made at school like clay animals and string designs, but no wicker thingamajig.

I dug around and finally pulled out a box from the farthest corner. It was gritty with dust, but I opened it anyway. It smelled musty, and I could see why. Sitting on top was a dried-up corsage that fell apart when I touched it. There was a sparkly crown, too, and underneath it pictures of Mom. The Homecoming Queen. Her expression was great, but the dress was all pinched in at the waist and sort of drooping off her shoulders, and her hair was jazzed up with fussy curls. Lifting up the photographs, I came across a notebook. I felt a little guilty but not enough to keep me from looking inside. There was page after page of poetry. Some of it about spring and sunsets and stuff like that, but most of it about love. It was really embarrassing. I felt as though I was reading my mother's mind, the way it used to be, before I was even born. I'd like to say that after a half-dozen or so of those poems my conscience got the better of me, but honestly, I stopped reading because I couldn't take any more on an empty (nearly) stomach. I jammed the notebook along the edge and was about to close the box when I noticed an even older-looking little book. I pulled it out. *Autographs,* it said. I didn't know Mom knew any famous people.

I looked inside. Mom's name was written in front, with the date, and grade 8. It was filled with names and little dumb rhymes, written in various scrawls. The pages were pink, yellow, blue, and white. The very last page said:

Way back here where no one will look
I'll write my name in your autograph book.
GERALD WINFIELD

61

Some pages just had signatures but there were a lot of dippy verses. One of them caught my attention:

> I wish you luck, I wish you joy,
> I wish you first a baby boy,
> And when his hair begins to curl,
> I wish you then a baby girl.
> ANNE K. JENNINGS

I read it again. The Anne K. Jennings who had wished that for Mom back in grammar school had been some kind of prophet. Joe came first, and he had curly hair. Then came baby girl Elaine. But what about me? There was nothing in that rhyme that hinted it would be a good idea to produce another girl child.

I slammed the book into the box and shoved it back into its corner. Where no one would look. Your crown and your photos and your autograph book. I could do dumb rhymes myself.

"Andrea, I just remembered—"

I jumped from surprise and, to hide my face, leaned over to brush off some dust.

"That horn thing got so moldy-looking we threw it out. "

"Oh, Mom." I dangled my dusty hands in front of me. "Then let's just make a pretty arrangement of colored candles."

"Let's." She kissed my forehead, and I

touched her shoulders with the upper, clean sides of my hands. I wish you luck, I thought. I wish you joy. And I hope you're glad, really glad, that you had me, too.

Mom was off on her timing, which meant that the vegetables got cooked before the turkey was brown. Finally she took it out, and I juggled things around in the oven, trying to keep them warm while she made gravy. Aunt Ellie was off in the living room, reaming out Uncle Herman for forgetting to bring the wine.

"Such a fuss," Mom said to me. "We have our own. Go ask Joe to take care of it."

"Didn't he go to pick up Cassie?"

"She can't come over after all. Get Joe now and tell the others we're about ready to eat."

I glanced into the living room and then headed for Joe's room. The door was open, and he was hunched on the edge of his bed. "It makes me wonder," he was saying.

Elaine was standing in front of the mirror, poking at a tiny zit on her chin. "Maybe she's just playing a little game."

"Cassie's not the game-playing type."

"Then take my advice—" Elaine caught my reflection. "What do *you* want?"

Joe straightened, and a mixture of emotions crossed his face.

"Sorry, but you're supposed to take care of the wine, Joe."

I glanced at Elaine, who was looking fairly decent for once in a dark blue dress. "And dinner's ready. We could use some help, you know. Like with carrying things out to the table."

Elaine heaved a sigh as she dragged past me. "I despise these family rituals."

"Joe . . ." I looked up as he draped an arm around my shoulder and moved me toward the door. "How come Cassie's not coming?"

"Tired. Too many flights too soon."

"Oh." That didn't seem to fit with what they'd been saying. Joe went to the kitchen, and I took away the one serving place too many that I'd put on the table.

The men and Aunt Ellie laughed it up a lot at dinner, but Mom looked dragged out. Joe didn't seem quite with it. Kitty stuffed her face even worse than I did, but Elaine picked at her food. Not only that but as soon as someone stopped eating, she snatched up the plate and rushed it out to the kitchen.

The grownups lingered at the table over coffee, and Joe helped Kitty and me carry out the rest of the stuff. "Just leave the leftovers on the counter," Mom called. "I'll take care of them later if you'll clean up the dishes."

"What a mess!" Elaine came from her room already changed into jeans and a turquoise embroidered top. "And for what?"

"You going somewhere, Elaine?" Kitty

forked up the last few string beans from a bowl. "You go out a lot, don't you?"

"Get with it, you guys," Elaine ordered. "Start scraping if you want me to help. I'm not hanging around here all day."

Kitty and I went to work, but suddenly I realized Elaine was over by the back door, talking to Joe. I marched over.

"Go see her," Elaine was saying in a low tone. "At least you'll know." She turned to me. "Oh, now what?"

"You're supposed to help."

"Sorry." She waved through the window at a van that had just pulled up. "Gotta leave." She grabbed her jacket and was gone.

Later on all of us sat around playing hearts, but after about an hour Joe said he was going out for a while.

We had a late dessert, and finally everyone went home.

I wanted to stay awake so I could ask Joe if he'd seen Cassie and how she was feeling, but I must have drifted off because I never did hear him come home.

In my humble opinion, kids should be treated like convalescents the first day back at school after a holiday. But some teachers take advantage of the natural weakened condition to strike a low blow.

Mr. Midlar, with what passed for him as a

smile, said, "Since you've had a full four days to review, this is a good time to see how much has sunk in." And sprang a quiz.

I was almost totally confused. Not only that. Mr. Midlar, pussyfooting down the aisles, paused at my desk even longer than usual. He did his toothy noises, which kept me from concentrating. When he did go back up to his desk, some guys who had finished their papers hung around and, without bothering to lower their voices, talked about college football games they'd seen over the weekend on TV. I hadn't finished the quiz when the bell rang.

By the time I got to study hall I was in no mood for the jab-jab routine of Kitty.

"Cut it out," I snarled over my shoulder.

"Did you get your copy of the *Junior Hi-Times?*"

"No."

"You ought to read the advice column in this issue." She started to shove the paper over my shoulder. I shoved it back. "I've already read it."

"How could you?" Her breath was like dragon fire on the back of my neck.

How could I say Robyn always let me read her columns in advance? "I mean, I don't need any advice." I heaved forward, thinking that besides a permanently polka-dotted back I'd end up the year with a spine like a pretzel.

I opened my math book to see what I'd

66

missed, but all I could see was the face of Mr. Midlar. Boy! Still taking it out on me on account of those run-ins with Miss Goof-Off Junction. He'd even put the beady eye on Robyn and tried to get her into trouble because of me.

Robyn! Iris! We could tell him off in the column, and everyone would know what kind of person they had on the teaching staff. I yanked a sheet of paper from my spiral and wrote:

DEAR IRIS:
I hate this teacher so much! He's picked on me from the very first day of school just because I remind him of someone who gave him a bad time. How can I prove I'm different? (Not that I honestly care that much, but I do care about getting a passing grade.)

D+ OR MAYBE D− STUDENT

P.S. He also has annoying habits.

I folded the letter up fast and stuck it into a book. During lunch hour I'd slip it to Robyn. I was sure she'd print it, out of friendship, if nothing else.

Two periods later I entered the howling arena known as the cafeteria. When I joined the group around Robyn, I found they were discussing, of all things, the Iris column.

"I just can't believe some of these letters,"

67

Lance Littinger was saying, elbows on the table, bending over the paper. "You guys, listen to this one." He leaned farther forward and read:

DEAR IRIS:
I did this really dumb thing. The hair on my arms is too dark, and I shaved it all off. Now I have a stubble. Am I supposed to keep shaving, or what?

BRUNETTE

"What did she answer?" Robyn asked, with an interested look.

Lance cleared his throat and read:

DEAR BRUNETTE:
You're not *supposed* to shave your arms, period. But since you did, let the hair grow back and then ask a beautician how to lighten it a little. In the meantime, do wear long sleeves.

"I can't believe," Judy Donath said, "that anyone would be dumb enough to do that. Shave, I mean. It sounds like a made-up letter to me. In fact"—she made a waving motion toward the paper—"I'll bet the whole column is a put-on. It might even have been written by an adult. A teacher."

"A teacher?" Sue asked.

"She may be right," Lance said. "These

68

answers are too know-it-all to have been written by a kid. I'll bet a teacher did the whole thing, and I know how we can check it out. Write a sizzler, and if it doesn't get printed, that's the tip-off. I can think of a gripe to write about right now.''

"What?" Robyn asked. "Did some seventh-grader refuse to give you her seat on the bus?''

"It says here," Judy read, "that there's a box in the library for the letters.'' She looked up and gave a grin that displaced her freckles. "Wouldn't it be hysterical if we griped about a teacher . . . and some teacher was actually writing the column?''

"No one would be stupid enough to put that kind of gripe into writing," Lance said. "It could kick back at you. Right between the teeth.''

My stomach lurched. It was as though Lance had read my mind. Or my note. This was a warning from on high, and I knew that as soon as the coast was clear I was going to ditch the evidence.

Later, out in the hall, Robyn drew me aside. "Wow, such a response! I'll bet from now on that box will be crammed with letters.'' She pulled at my arm. "Where are you going?''

"I've got to get rid of something.''

She followed me to the trash can, keeping up a line of talk.

I reached into my top book. And then the

next. And then the other. "Robyn!" I could feel my heart flopping as my fingers fumbled through the books again. "I . . . can't find it."

"Find what?"

I put my books on the floor and one by one held them up by the bindings. "I've lost it!" Now my heart was jumping like crazy. I picked up the books and faced Robyn. "It was a letter to you. I mean, Iris."

"Shhhh." She glanced around. "What did it say?"

"Just how much I hate Mr. Midlar. Well, I didn't mention him by name, but anyone would guess."

Robyn's green eyes caught and held my look. "You surely didn't sign it?"

"No."

"Well, you'd better just pray that whoever picks up your letter pitches it."

"They probably won't." The beating had stopped. Maybe I was dead. I felt dead.

Robyn put her free hand around my shoulder and started me down the hall. "Don't look so guilty. Whoever finds it isn't going to know who wrote it. Kids recognize only their best friends' handwriting."

I nodded and managed a weak smile. But as Robyn swung off, a sudden thought made me sag against the wall. Teachers recognized handwriting. It was an acquired talent. And I could have dropped that note in the lunchroom!

7

The only way I survived the afternoon without falling apart was by telling myself that I might have—I could have—stopped by my locker and shoved the note inside for safekeeping. It wasn't much to hang onto, but it was all I had.

When the last bell rang, I zeroed down the hall, shakingly worked the combination, rattled the door open, and scrambled through the stuff.

Of course, no note.

Robyn, when I needed her most, was off somewhere in conference.

The hall was deserted by the time I finally shoved everything back and slammed the locker shut.

Suddenly a hand clamped on my shoulder. "Where do you think you're going?"

My joints absolutely locked. Then, from my paralyzed brain came the message: *Boy's voice, dummy. Boy.*

I turned, still in shock. It was that—uh—Chris. Chris Walker.

He smiled. "Didn't mean to scare you. Can't you make the meeting?"

"Meeting . . . ?"

"Yeah. You know. For the play."

"Oh. For the play." I couldn't get myself together. "You're the one who's doing—uh—"

"Lights and some sound. Wondered if you had anything special in mind? Like, is your crew going to do the dogs howling, or should I record it for you?"

It was all going too fast for me. First, the fear, then the questions, then through it all the thought. And this just killed me. He's—*wow*.

"I . . . haven't thought that far." To tell the honest truth, I hadn't thought even into the opening scene. And here was this Chris, seeking me out, treating me like some authority.

"So how about the meeting?"

"Sure. I can make it. It just slipped my mind." I turned and headed for the auditorium, trying to act unconcerned, and he strolled beside me.

"Look, I didn't mean to pressure you."

"No sweat. As I said, I just forgot."

"I know how that goes." He smiled in a general sort of way, and all I can say is that it was like sunshine after a soggy spring day. His hair, just beyond blond, was curly. Not deep

72

curly and trimmed like Joe's, but lifting in a
rounded look, almost like a cherub's. I had no
idea of the color of his eyes behind that smiling
look, but they were probably in the blue department. "Do you like working with sound?"
I asked, to break the silence and to give me a
chance to pull myself together.

"Sound and lights. Sure, it's fun if there's
any kind of challenge. The routine stuff, like
for PTA meetings, is a drag."

When we entered the auditorium, the few
people down front turned to look when Chris
and I came down the aisle.

"Oh, there you are," Mrs. Vidal said in that
gleeful voice of hers. "Our two key people."
She gave a little laugh and tilted her head at the
others. "I didn't mean that you're not important, but this particular show depends a lot on
mood and spooky effects, and Chris here, and
Andrea, are going to make it all happen."

She hopes, I thought.

Chris, hands in jeans pockets, sank into a
theater seat, and I, tossing aside my ski jacket,
scooted into a seat across the aisle.

"We've been talking about some specific
problems in doing this play," Mrs. Vidal said.
"Do you have your crew lined up yet, Andrea?"

"Well, actually—not exactly."

"Could you let me know soon?"

"Sure." As soon as I get my life sorted out.

73

"I don't mean to rush any of you, but the Christmas holidays will be here before we know it"—Mrs. Vidal made a little *tch* sound to go along with her grin as the kids reacted—"and after that we'll really have to dig in. I know April seems a long way away, but since we have to work around other activities, and only an hour or so at a time . . ."

"I don't get what it is we're supposed to be doing right now," Ben Hoenig said.

"As set construction head, I'd like you to make up a floor plan of the stage. Mr. Warner in industrial arts will help," Mrs. Vidal answered.

"Where are we going to get Dracula's costume?" Candy Burkett asked. "It's for sure I'm not going to make it, and neither will my mother."

"Let's worry about that later," Mrs. Vidal said, sounding a shade like Scarlett O'Hara. "Just work up costume sketches for all the characters. Any other questions?" She glanced at her bracelet watch. I had the feeling she was eager to get home to her husband and probably start dinner.

I felt I ought to ask a question, but I couldn't remember anything specific from the script. I'd only read it through once.

Chris drawled out, "Andrea and I are going to get together to work out some of the effects. They've gotta be coordinated."

I must be blessed with a vivid imagination because those simple words made me flush.

"Super," Mrs. Vidal said, gathering her things. "We'll have another meeting soon, then."

Walking home, with the collar of my navy ski jacket pulled up against the November chill, I was only vaguely conscious of slogging through soggy leaves, mired in mud. Did people really fall in love at first sight? But I'd seen Chris before. First *sound*, then. It wasn't only his looks, which, to use Mrs. V.'s favorite word, were super, but his voice. So calm, so assured. So friendly. Friendly. That was the operative word. He was friendly to me because he was a friendly person. Was he more than friends with some girl at school? I had no idea.

And stop thinking in those directions, I told myself, kicking at a pile of leaves and almost taking a skid. He has a job to do with the play, and my job sort of dovetails with his. That's all there is to it.

Don't let it be, I thought. Let it be more than that. Let it be that he thinks you're . . . what? Pretty? Duh. Intelligent? Huh. Capable? Maybe it was capable. I hadn't *said* anything to prove I wasn't. In fact, I *was* capable, once I got going. But big whip. Capable is pretty low on the scale of what a guy is looking for in a girl.

I noticed that besides being chilly, the air was also gray, with a darkening look of fog to come. I hate fog worse than any other kind of weather. They say English women have terrific complexions because of dampish weather, but I'd as soon do without it and put my skin into the hands of the cosmetic industry.

As the chill crept into my bones a deeper chill from inside me stirred and made me start to shake.

Mr. Midlar. I'd forgotten. How could I have forgotten? Was he at this moment huddled in his wretched quarters (not wretched meaning *poor*, but because he occupied them) with my note smoothed out on a table in front of him? I could see him, blinking, sucking air in through his teeth, turning over one homework paper after another, checking various handwritings against that on the note. He zooms in for a closer look! And his eyes gleam like penlights as he sees Andrea Marshall's paper. Ah-ha! That's it! The matching handwriting!

If that happened, *when* it happened, Midlar would be convinced I was even worse than my sister. At least she'd fought him face to face.

What could I do?

Wait, I guess. Wait and see.

No, I had to talk it out with someone. Someone adult, who could help.

Joe? Joe wasn't easy to reach any more.

Dad was calm and easy to talk to, but he worked so hard, and sometimes so late . . .

Mom.

It gave me a jolt to discover that my very own mom was my third choice. I realize that lots of girls my age are on the outs with their mothers. It wasn't that way with us, though. When Mom yelled at me it was mostly out of frustration with Elaine. But that wasn't fair. She ought to look at me too, as a person, and realize I had problems also, and needs. Mom just never realized how much I needed her.

I scuffed up to the front door. Why didn't she?

I went inside, took off my sloshy shoes, and listened. No scream sessions today, no stereo. "Mother?"

"Out here in the kitchen."

She sounded alone. Maybe . . . maybe she would even *welcome* this chance to talk to me. Not that she was going to be thrilled by the note I'd written, but she might be delighted to have someone ask her advice for a change. She'd probably come up with a simple answer that would solve everything and after that I could mention Chris. Casually, because Mom's a born romantic, and I wouldn't want her getting any ideas.

I pitched my stuff onto my bed and went to the bathroom to wash off mud streaks.

"I'll be there in a minute," I called out to Mom in the kitchen. No, thinking it over, I wouldn't mention Chris. All these years Mom had been waiting to relive her own fun times

77

of proms, pom-pom, and homecoming things through her beautiful elder daughter. But that hadn't happened. I couldn't pretend I was going to make up for what Mom had missed. Besides, right now the topic was the note and what to do about it.

I dried my hands, got as far as the kitchen doorway, said, "Mom, I really need your—" and stopped.

She was standing smack in the middle of the room, arms at her sides, with a puzzled look on her face. For a crazy moment I thought she was playing the part of one of those TV housewives, trying to decide which half of the room had been waxed with Brand X.

"What's up?" I asked.

"I just can't figure it out."

I glanced around. No clue. "Figure what out?"

"Why she withdrew all her money from the bank."

"Withdrew? Who? You mean Elaine?"

"Every cent."

"Oh." I might have known. Elaine. Always Elaine. I went to the refrigerator and found a square tin with a hunk of fruit Jell-O clinging for dear life to one corner. I took it and began eating, right from the pan. So much for my problems. "Why did she take out her money?"

"Andrea, I just told you I don't know why."

Mom pushed up the sleeves of her tan sweater and pulled them down again. "We got our bank statements today. Your dad used to fuss because they got strewn around, so lately I've been putting them on his dresser so he can record the interest for income tax. Oh, never mind all that. The point is, Elaine's statement read *zero*."

"She'll have a fit when she finds out you opened her envelope."

"What does she want with all that cash?" Mom ran a hand down her cheek.

"Maybe new clothes."

"Two hundred and sixty-three dollars' worth? The things she wears you could buy for loose change at a garage sale."

"Maybe she wants to buy a car."

"Car? Car? With that piddling amount of money?"

First huge, now piddling. "Maybe . . ." I couldn't think of anything. "Isn't she home yet?"

Mom turned and looked at me, really looked at me for the first time since I'd entered the room. "Andrea," she said, "would I be standing here talking to you if Elaine were home?"

There was silence, twenty-five cubic feet of it, between us. I looked at my mother. "No," I said then. "I guess you wouldn't."

She didn't even get it. "Well, then," she said with a little frown and left the room.

8

I dialed Robyn. Feeling so alone and empty, I needed to hear another human voice.

"What's the word?" she asked.

"Depends on the subject." Like flash cards, possibilities popped into my mind. Midlar/terror. Chris/angel. Mom/void. Elaine/disgust. I chose disgust.

"Elaine's at it again. Took all her money out of the bank, more than two hundred, and Mom's in a catatonic state."

"Why did she do that? Elaine?"

"Who knows? She gives me a pain."

"Maybe she's pg."

"Pregnant!"

"That much money. You know?"

"I don't know." I felt sick. "I don't want to talk about it."

"Okay, choose another subject."

Again, the flash cards. The hurt with Mom was too fresh. And Chris. I wasn't ready to share that dreamlike subject, even with Robyn. *Midlar*. "I still didn't find that Iris letter. If I dropped it in the cafeteria, and *he* picked it up . . . !"

"Don't be manic-depressive. Couldn't an S.O.T.E. have found it just as easily?" S.O.T.E. was Robyn's short cut for kids who were Scum of the Earth.

"Thanks a lot. That's real cheering. You know what a Scum would do. Pass it around."

"Andy, my pet, you really are heading in the manic-depressive direction. Can't you snap out of it and think of something positive?"

"You mean, like the results of Elaine's rabbit test?"

"I just mentioned she could be."

"Well, she probably is. She's done everything else there is to get attention." I slammed a cupboard drawer shut. "But I don't want to talk about her."

Robyn was silent, and I realized that, after all, I was the one who had called her. "We had a crew meeting after school." I could give myself the pleasure of talking about the subject and yet keep Chris secret. "I've got to find someone to help me" (besides *him*) "and begin getting organized. I guess I'll start reading through the script and making notes tonight." (Then I'll have a legit reason to talk to him.)

"I wish I could help, but . . ."

"That's all right." I was very fond of Robyn,

but what I wanted now on my crew was some-one dull, plain. Creepy. Too bad Kitty was al-ready in the cast. "I'm going to start right now, in fact. See you tomorrow."

"Right."

I read through the play and noted the special effects as follows:

Howling of dogs
Special music when Dracula enters the scene
French doors that open and close by them-
    selves
Fog rolling into the room
Bats flying in and out of the room
Chair that moves by itself
Lights that flash on with a wave of Dracula's
    hand

God. What had I let myself in for. Bats? Flying? In the back of the book was this big hot suggestion that the things could be carved of balsa wood, with wire and cloth wings at-tached "in such a way as to permit flapping motion as the bat swoops across the stage." Dandy. That cleared it up just fine. I felt sick to my stomach.

Next I checked off the effects that might fall into Chris' department. Dogs howling, music, lights. Fog? It said to do it with dry ice, dropped into water. My job, I supposed, along with the moving chair and French doors. And the blasted bats.

After dinner, I'd call around and find someone to help.

Dinner? As though on cue, my stomach rumbled. I opened my door. No kitchen sounds, no cooking smells. Putting the script on the bed, face down, as a reminder, I went out to the hall. Mom's bedroom door was closed. Was she asleep, I wondered? If she was in there crying, she was certainly being quiet about it. Whatever, I didn't feel like being rebuffed again. As for dinner, there was always Ptomaine Junction, over by the stoplights.

With the cold gray fingers of depression coming at me again, I decided to duck down to the basement to my little land of isolation, where the only worry was a question of balance.

Downstairs, I got into my old beat-up leotard and tights and did limbering-up exercises. As the warmth flooded my body the tensions melted away. I did a forward roll mount onto the beam, a one-leg squat, a step, turn, and a few other movements. I felt free and weightless, like in those dreams where you're lifting and floating, only here I was in control. Forward, forward, balance, then a back walkover, ending in an arabesque, arms outflung, triumphant. This was it—the one place I felt fully alive. *Joe, Joe, look at me!*

I went through the simple routines we'd done

at school and then worked on some of the more complex moves Joe had helped me learn. "Now, touch me if you need to," he used to say. Finally a little quivering in my thighs warned me I was overdoing it, so I did a front vault dismount, picked up my towel, and sitting cross-legged on the mat, mopped up the sweat.

It was eerie, the way Joe's voice kept coming back to me. It could have been because we'd spent so many hours working out down here together, or maybe it was because with all the other stuff batting around in my brain lately he'd been squeezed out of my thoughts. Anyway, I could almost hear him saying once again, "Elaine shouldn't hang by her knees unless she can pull herself up again." That was way last summer.

"On the unevens? Where would she do that?" I'd asked with a stupid stare.

"Symbolically speaking, twerp. She does these daredevil things, then when she can't pull herself out of them, yells for help. Some day there'll be no one around to hear her."

His voice was so clear in my mind, it gave me the chills. I could almost literally hear Elaine belting away. With the towel wrapped around my shoulders, I got up from the mat and walked toward my clothes, then instead went over and flung open the door. Ah-ha! I wasn't freaking out after all. Sister was home.

Yelling. Mom had come out to do battle, and I could even hear Dad, though not too clearly.

I went up and found they were in Elaine's room, all standing, because actually there was no decent place to sit.

"Pregnant!" Elaine screamed. I flinched. Wow. Had Mom heard Robyn? I didn't think so.

"We're only asking," Dad said. "We have a right to know."

"Thanks a lot! Thanks a whole bunch," Elaine lashed out. "It's really great to know my parents have such trust in me!" She unknotted a plaid shirt at the waist, peeled it from the matching T-shirt, and flung it into a corner.

"It's not a question of trust!" Mom said, sounding unstrung.

"Boy, you're really jumping to conclusions, though, aren't you?" She kicked off her shoes in the direction of the closet. "I withdrew my money, my very own money, so naturally you think the worst. You don't give me any credit at all, do you?"

"Credit for what?"

"For being able to manage my own life."

"So far you haven't shown the slightest sign, and besides, young lady, you're only—" Mom's voice started rising.

"Lucille. Calm down." Dad started to move some things aside to sit down but thought better of it. "I don't know how these simple discussions always turn into scenes."

I knew, all right. As the saying goes, "The best defense is offense." Elaine does it all the time and it works. It was working now.

"Honey, we really want to understand you," Mom said. "Can't we talk calmly?"

"Oh, sure, calmly. You come in here and accuse me of all kinds of things and then expect me to be calm and happy about it. Well, let me tell you something. I'm sick of your checking up on my every move. I wish you'd leave me alone. Why don't you both just get off my case!"

Elaine slammed onto the bench in front of her dressing table and with her forearm swept a bunch of junk to the floor. Something broke.

Mom started to leap forward, but Dad grabbed her arm. "Leave it."

"I'm sick and tired of this place!" Elaine shouted into the mirror. "I'm sick and tired of everything!"

"You're not as sick as we are!" I said, glaring at her reflection.

Elaine whirled around. "What the hell do *you* want?"

"I just want—" I looked at Mom and Dad and faltered. "I just want my . . . dinner."

"God!" Elaine's look traveled over my body. I realized how I must look in my sweaty workout clothes. "The world could be ready to collapse and you'd say, 'Hand me the cat-sup.' "

"*Please*. I'd say *please*. Besides, jerk, the world isn't about to collapse just because you're upset."

Elaine jumped up, face flushed and eyes blazing. "Get out!"

"That's enough." Dad gave Elaine a warning look and sort of motioned Mom and me out of the room.

The door slammed behind the three of us.

We stood there like dopes and looked at each other.

"What *did* she want the money for?" I asked.

"We never quite got that question answered," Dad said, with a twist of his lips. "And frankly, at this moment I'm just too worn out to pursue it."

It was only a few minutes later that we heard the front door slam and the sound of a car taking off.

"She didn't have time to use the phone," Dad said. "What does she do, send out smoke signals?"

I opened the refrigerator, a reflex action with me. "Don't you get it? She was going out all along. She pulled that big final scene just to get rid of you."

Dad stared. Mom looked beat.

"Why don't you two go out somewhere for dinner?" I suggested.

"Good idea," Dad said. "But what about you?"

"I'm on a diet."

"Since when?"

"I have to start sometime. Before the holidays."

Mom put her fingers to her temples. "Don't mention the holidays."

"All right." But they were coming.

After they left I had soup and a one-slice-of-bread sandwich. To keep my mind off any further food I decided to watch TV in my room and thumb through the script again during commercials.

I went into Mom and Dad's room to borrow the portable set. I was just leaning down to unplug it when I saw a paper lying on the floor. It looked like a poem, and it was in Mom's handwriting. I put it back on the table by her lounge chair, but the lines just sort of reached out and stopped me. I started reading, and then my hands trembled. I had to blink to keep the lines from waving:

Has anyone seen my daughter, my delight?
You will know her by the star-sparkle of her
    eyes.

Her eyes are blue velvet with light shining
   through
and they glow with the joy of youth.

Her hair, a cascade of chestnut, flings back
against her shoulders when she laughs
that special laugh
that warms my soul.
But she is gone. She's gone away.
A stranger came.
She stares at me with stone-cold gaze.
Her lips curl not with laughter, but with cruel
   phrase.

Won't someone please bring back my daugh-
   ter . . .
My darling?
My life.

I was blubbering by the time I came to the
last line, and I left everything and rushed into
my room where I sobbed into my pillow.

I could forgive Mom for loving Elaine more
than she did me. She couldn't help it. Any more
than I could help loving Joe more than—well,
not my parents—but anyone. But I'd never,
never forgive Elaine for what she was doing
with that love—tearing it right out of Mom and
flinging it into her face!

Finally I stopped sobbing, blew my nose, and
sat up. When had Mom written those lines?
This afternoon probably.

Well, I could write a poem too, expressing my sentiments. It certainly wasn't going to be a love poem.

I grabbed a piece of paper, and as though possessed, wrote without even stopping to think.

ELAINE
You think you're so super,
Elaine.
The world's your domain,
Elaine.
What you don't realize,
Little Pretty Blue Eyes,
Is you're not all that great
With your temper and hate
And you give me a pain,
Elaine.

9

In spite of no one in our family really caring all that much, the Christmas holidays were coming at us like a snorting locomotive.

Being short of ready cash as per usual, I leaped at Rosemary's suggestion that I help out at the florist shop after school some nights and on Saturdays.

It was pure chaos in the back room with box after box of artificial decorative stuff, plus about a zillion live plants. My job was to see that the main room was kept supplied with wrapping paper and cards and ribbons, and to fill in wherever the need was desperate. Rosemary worked nights, concocting arrangements of candles, pine cones, greenery, and ribbons, which disappeared off the display counter within days.

Among the glitter and dazzle my favorite things were the weathered wood boxes (they were fake weathered, of course) with a little, speckled brown bird sitting on sprays of natural-toned dried weeds and cones. On the other hand, I never tired of staring at one special wreath in the main room. It was a soft though shimmery silver, with old rose ribbons and sachets and silk roses of various shades of pink. It reminded me of the *Nutcracker Suite*, and fairy tales and a world that never was except in the dreams of far-off childhood. It cost forty-five dollars.

Home, by contrast, was *Bleak House*. Mom hardly bothered to clean, much less decorate. "There's time," she said one evening when I suggested hauling the holiday things out of the closet to take stock. "And besides, I don't need all that stuff littering up the place just now."

"What do you want for Christmas?" I asked, partly to cheer her up and partly to get her motivated.

"What do I want? My sanity." She kicked off a loafer and rubbed her foot on the rug to get rid of an itch. "What do you want?"

I shrugged. "Mom, why don't you get your hair cut?"

"Why don't you?" She grinned.

"Because I'm young!" Great. That was just the greatest thing to say. "I mean, it doesn't matter with me. But if you had your hair styled you'd look . . ."

"What?"

"I mean it would give you a lift." I tried a

smile. "Maybe it would help bring back your sanity."

"The only thing that would bring back my sanity is—"

I knew what she was thinking. For Elaine to shape up.

". . . is a miracle."

I didn't think we could count on that happening. Ever since the big flare-up Elaine had been like a mean-eyed shadow, coming and going and speaking, when she absolutely had to speak, in a monotone. Creep.

At school things were in the usual preholiday state, with kids goofing off and teachers looking as though they needed a vacation worse than anyone.

Nothing at all happened about that note I wrote about Midlar. His attitude toward me in class was neither worse nor better.

"There's been no talk from the kids about it," I said one day to Robyn, "and you say it hasn't shown up in the box in the library. So what could have happened to it?"

"Swept out with the trash," Robyn said. At least she didn't say the *rest* of the trash.

I turned my attention to the problem of getting a crew member for the play who would be no competition in the Chris line, and solved it by choosing a boy. Ken Petit lived down the street from us. We were on fair terms because we'd known each other for years. Also, he had the added attraction of having a father with loads of power equipment in his garage. You could hear his buzz saw going into all hours of the night during the summer if the air conditioning wasn't running.

Ken said if I'd draw up a design, he'd get his father to pick up the balsa wood and carve out the bat bodies. And glory be, when I did dig up some books on bats at the library and showed Ken's dad how the wings were riblike, almost on the principle of an umbrella, he said he could construct them by soldering wires together. It just goes to show that if you find the right people to help with the right thing you're home free.

On the Chris situation there wasn't any person to ask.

One day in study hall—a quiet day, Kitty was home with a cold—I amused myself by writing a pretend letter to Iris.

DEAR IRIS:
I like this boy so much, but he doesn't know it. He was friendly one time, and I thought it was me. But nothing since. So I guess he's just after my brains (joke) to help put a project across that we're working on—or supposed to be working on—together. He's very serious about this venture. What can I do to get him to notice me as a girl?

BAFFLED

I didn't even realize the bell had rung until I noticed kids shuffling past toward the exits. I ripped up the letter, stuffed it into my English lit book, and followed the crowd.

This was, as it happened, publication day of the *Junior Hi-Times*, and kids swept up their free copies from the stack on their way to the cafeteria.

Robyn rushed me through the line. "Come on, I want to hear reactions. The last you-know-what is a gas, and I didn't even have to make it up."

I'll say this for Robyn, she put on a better performance that noon than I have ever seen in a class play. "Really!" she said. "Read that last letter again, I can't believe it!"

In fact, everyone was carrying on about the letters including me, and that's because I was doing a little acting of my own. I had noticed Chris coming into the lunchroom, and I thought he looked over toward our table now and then, but of course, we were one of the noisiest groups in the whole room.

There was so much going on, we were late leaving. I glanced Chris's way and nearly died when he smiled and motioned to me.

"I have to talk to someone," I said to Robyn, my voice croaking.

She walked on, hardly noticing. Fame, even anonymous fame, must do something to people.

Chris took back his tray. (In our school leaving a tray on the table is a capital crime.) "I've been looking around for you," he said, out in the hall.

Same here. "Don't you always eat in the cafeteria?" *I never see you. I've looked. Wow, have I looked.*

"Usually, I carry lunch and eat in the audio-visual department. I'm helping Mr. Keenan put together some sound for his church group. Some pageant."

"Oh."

Chris reached into his jacket pocket. "I thought you might like to have this back." He held out a folded note.

I felt my knees creak like smashed Styrofoam, and blood scalded my cheeks. My note! But hadn't I torn it up? Was I losing my memory? My fingers felt the edge of my lit book, but I didn't dare open it.

"Well?" He smiled that slow smile. "Don't you want it back?"

"How"—my lips didn't want to move— "how do you know it's mine?"

"I saw you drop it on your way into the lunchroom. I was going to give it to you, but you jumped in with your friends, and I didn't want to embarrass you. In case, you know, it was something . . . you know. "

Boy-girl. Again, I felt the flush. Then, suddenly, dawn broke, as they say, and I gasped.

"You mean you found my note about . . ." I didn't even dare mention his name.

"Yeah. I hate to admit I forgot about it. I felt it in my shirt pocket a little while ago. Sorry it missed today's issue."

"I'm not!" I took the note, and my hands were so damp I could hardly rip the paper. "This thing could have got me into lots of trouble." I stuck the scraps in a book.

He smiled. "Then it's a good thing I found it instead of someone else. Aren't you glad I kind of keep an eye on you?"

I didn't know what to say to that. He was kidding, of course. And I hated the flush I could feel rising to my cheeks that might make him think I thought he meant it.

"I—uh—have been working on the special effects."

"The what? Oh, for *Dracula*. Good. We'll have to get together in January and compare notes. Well, see you."

Walking away, I consoled myself with the thought that we'd meet in January. I could live on that. As for the note, I didn't even mind the misery it had caused. Today more than made up for it. Even if Chris was kidding about keeping his eye on me.

When I got home, I went into Elaine's room to get a packet of matches. Among other things, she smoked like a campfire. It struck me as a bit strange that I could see the entire carpet. Usually there were just patches of it showing between clumps of clothes. There weren't even any half-emptied bottles of Coke on her dresser, and, for that matter, only a few nearly used-up yukky make-up containers. There ought to be a letter to Santa, I thought, finding a packet with three matches left in it. *Dear Santa: I have been a good girl and cleaned up my room.*

I went to the kitchen, and using two different saucers (no mixing Chris with Midlar), I set the notes on fire. I also read the note from Mom: "Honey, Rosemary is swamped, so I'm helping out again. I'll probably work late, so please call your dad, and if he's coming home for dinner, cook something for the three of you. Love, Mom."

I didn't mind, but since when was it taken for granted I was supposed to cook for Miss Sulks?

Dad said, when I called, that as long as Mom wasn't going to be home, he'd stay over too. "It seems everyone in town has decided this is Physical Fitness Year, so we're really doing business," he said.

"Isn't that good?"

"It's wonderful. I just hope we can keep up on stock. We still have shipments coming in from the manufacturers, with the usual delays. How are things at home?"

"Quiet."

"Is Elaine there?"

"Is she ever?"

"Honey, if you don't want to eat alone . . ."

"I don't mind. Remember, I'm on a diet."

"Don't overdo it. I like you just the way you are."

"That's fine, Dad, but it can't be just you and me against the world of the skinnys." Oh, wow. "I mean, at my age, I have to think of those inches."

"Forget inches," Dad said kiddingly. "We're into the metric system."

"Ha-ha. See you later, Dad."

I possibly wouldn't have thought about being lonesome if Dad hadn't mentioned it, but the house suddenly seemed so empty and dreary that even favorite rock numbers on the kitchen radio didn't cut it. I dialed Robyn, but she was about to go Christmas shopping. She and her parents were going to Florida for the holidays. I wondered if she'd buy me something, and that brought me to the thought of making up my own shopping list.

While I was eating tomato soup and a bunch of raw vegetables (which only built up my appetite for a sandwich), I jotted down possibilities for family and friends.

Mom—gift coupon for a beauty appointment.
  (Would she feel glad or insulted????????)

Dad—?????
Joe—sweater? (Too expensive probably)
Elaine—

I could think of all kinds of things for Elaine, like a Do I Have a Winning Personality self-quiz kit or a course in a charm school. Or maybe perpetual maid service. Only she practically had that now.

The phone rang. "Joe!"

"Hi, toots. What are you doing?"

"Making out my Christmas list."

"Yeah? What do you want?"

"Me?"

"You used to make out a list a mile long. Remember the year you asked for a cat?"

"I didn't get it."

"You still want it?"

"Dunno. What do you want?"

"To be five years older."

"You will be." (But so would Cassie.) "What are you giving yor true love? A diamond ring?"

"Don't be dumb."

"What's dumb about it?"

"Do I seem like a guy who'd gift-wrap himself? Besides . . ."

"Besides what?"

"What makes you think Cassie'd want to be engaged to me?"

"Why wouldn't she?"

100

"Let's scrap that subject and get back to the animal kingdom. You still want a fluffy white cat?"

"It wouldn't have to be white or fluffy. I'd settle for anything. This empty house is giving me the creeps."

"Folks working again?"

"Yep. And Elaine's nowhere in sight. As usual. Not that she's any company. When are you coming home?"

"Four days before Christmas. Tuesday. You're wondering why I called?"

"To cheer your esteemed relative. Me."

"And to see what you thought of the idea of the three of us going in together to get the folks something really nice. I don't know what, but if we pooled our money we could go beyond the usual rinkydink presents."

"Okay. I'll mention it to Elaine. But . . ."

"But what?"

"Nothing." There was no point in running up Joe's phone bill telling how Elaine had taken all her money out of the bank. Besides, it just at this moment occurred to me that she might have done it for Christmas shopping, though if she had, why the four-star scene? "Joe, I'll be thinking. And I'll see you in a couple of weeks."

I finished my gift list with a possible album for Robyn and candleholders to mail to both sets of grandparents, and then started in on my homework. Now that I was beginning to gain on some of my grades I found it was easier to keep up.

When the folks finally got home, they looked tired, but cheerful. Money in the pocket and all that.

We were having coffee and hot chocolate in the living room, talking about things at Rosemary's and at Dad's shop, and plans for Christmas, when Mom looked at her watch and frowned. "When did Elaine say she'd be back?"

"I haven't seen her."

Mom set down her cup. "Even after school?"

"She hasn't been around. But her room's clean."

"That's odd." Mom got up and went to Elaine's room.

"You ought to lay down the law to her," I said to Dad. "Even Joe didn't come and go the way Elaine does, without a word. You'd think this was some kind of hotel."

"George?" Mom's voice sounded strange. "Would you come here?"

Dad got up and so did I.

"What's wrong?" he asked, going into Elaine's room, with me right behind him.

Mom was standing at the opened closet door, her eyes wide and staring.

"What's the matter?"

"Her . . . knapsack is gone. So are some of her clothes. Oh, George . . ." She reached out. Dad grabbed her.

"Are you sure?"

"She's gone!" Mom gave a rattling sob. "Elaine has gone! Gone!"

10

The worst part about those next two days was not knowing. Mom called kids Elaine knew, but they all claimed they didn't have a clue to her whereabouts. Dad checked out the cab company, but they had no record, and the bus, train, and airline services couldn't give any help.

"She's lying in a ditch somewhere, dead!" Mom shrieked once. Why a ditch, I didn't know. I guess that's what parents say.

"Lucille, you've got to pull yourself together," Dad told her. "The police have a complete description, and if anything had happened, we'd hear about it. It's just a matter of waiting until she contacts us."

They made me go to school, for all the good it did me, and afterwards I had to go help Rosemary. Mom was sitting by the phone when I left in the morning, and still there when I returned. A couple of neighbors kept popping in to console her. Dad dashed home every noon and whenever else he could get away. The timing couldn't have been worse for Dad, but of course that hadn't entered Elaine's head. The folks wouldn't call Joe. "He can't do anything, and there's no use upsetting him," they said. I didn't agree.

Finally, on the third day, Mom called me at the florist shop.

"She's all right," she said. "Elaine. I just talked to her."

"Wow. Where is she?"

"In Arizona."

"Arizona!"

"With Steve. I could just clobber her!"

"How'd she get way out there?"

"Hitchhiked. *Hitchhiked*. She's just crazy, that's all. After she got far enough so she thought she couldn't be traced, she took a bus. Andrea, why does your sister do these things? What have I done wrong?"

"Have you called Dad?"

"Of course!"

"Is he going out to get her?"

"Going out . . . ? But we don't know where she is!"

"You just said Arizona."

"That's a *state*. She wouldn't say where. Just that she's with Steve, and she's okay, and she doesn't want us to worry."

That's my sister. All heart. "Well, Mom,

105

there's nothing you can do then until she makes up her mind to come home."

"If."

Let her stay, I felt like saying.

Rosemary snorted when I gave her the flash about Elaine. "I didn't doubt for a minute that she was all right. That girl's too mean to get hurt," she said, wiring a big red bow on a potted poinsettia. "Sorry. I guess I shouldn't say that."

"Why not? It's the truth." But I would have felt a lot better if Elaine had asked for a return airline ticket. "I wonder if she'll come back for Christmas?"

"Depends upon what she's into. What does this Steve do for a living?"

I shrugged.

Rosemary took off her smock and reached for her coat. "I'm going to drive you home. I have the feeling your mom needs to get her arms around someone."

"Now? Why now? She's relieved."

"Trust me."

Mom grabbed me the minute I walked into the house, and it was like childhood revisited. She just wouldn't let go. "Oh, baby, don't you ever leave me. It would break my heart."

I knew very well it was my sister Mom was crying about, but to tell the truth, I felt needed even though I realized I was only the stand-in.

106

"Can we call Joe now?"

"I suppose we should."

"He has a right to know. Besides, he might come up with an idea of how to trace her."

Joe didn't seem all that excited about the news. "There's no way she's going to come back until it suits her purposes. So, Mom, just play it easy. I'll try to get home early for the holidays."

The three of us, Mom, Dad, and I, kept busy, but there was always the hollowness in the house at night. And the phone that didn't ring. When Joe got home Monday evening (his one Tuesday class had been canceled), we still hadn't done anything about a Christmas tree.

"What kind do you want?" he asked Mom. "Andy and I will go out to get it if you can spare the car."

"A big one," Mom said. "For the front bay window." Something, I thought, that Elaine will see the minute she turns the corner when she returns.

"Want to come along?" Joe asked.

"No." Mom glanced toward the phone. "I'll just wait here."

On Wednesday, when I was off school, Joe and I went shopping. Nothing was said about the two of us going in together for gifts. I ended up getting Mom a cologne and bath powder combo, Dad a crossword-puzzle reference book, and Joe a long cable-knit beige and brown muffler. "I guess I should get something for Elaine," I told Joe when we rejoined.

"Yeah, as an act of faith."

"Huh?"

"Meaning, we expect her."

I got her an album of music from the ballet, partly to improve her taste, and partly to preserve my hearing. "If she doesn't like it, I'll take it back, for when I get my own stereo," I told Joe.

"That's what I like about you. Always thinking ahead." Joe stopped me at the jewelry counter. He blinked and made a funny little gesture with his mouth when he looked at the rings. Then he steered me toward the door.

"What *are* you going to buy Cassie?"

"Haven't decided yet."

"You haven't seen her since you've been home, have you?"

"She's on a flight," he said quickly. "Maybe she'll come over to the house on Christmas Eve. That is, if she hasn't any other plans."

Cassie did come over, with a whole shopping bag full of gifts and a fancy box of chocolates she'd picked up in New York. I was glad that at the last minute I'd rushed out and bought her a silky scarf.

We sat around drinking eggnog and listening to carols and pretending not to listen for the

108

phone. Mom had on a hot pink hostess gown that Dad had given her as a pre-present, and she'd done the complete make-up bit. Only it just lay there, with no expression to back it up.

Dad got a little high (he kept slipping out to the kitchen for what he called some "real stuff"), and the evening dragged on.

"Shall we open the presents?" I finally asked.

Mom glanced at her watch. "It's early."

Early! It was nearly midnight.

"I still have an errand to run," Joe said, getting up. "Why don't we put off the family gift exchange until tomorrow?"

I glanced at Cassie, looking more angelic than ever in a powder-blue knit. Was that relief on her pretty face?

"I have plans for tomorrow," she said, "so . . ." She kissed all of us and murmured things about good holidays. Everyone, I noticed, avoided the word "happy."

After they left, the rest of us started off to bed.

"Don't . . ." Mom said, as Dad started to lock the front door.

Before I fell into bed, Mom came in and held me so close I felt welded to her. "My precious," she said. "My baby." Finally, with a sigh, she left.

I was drugged with sleep, or maybe eggnog,

when I felt someone sitting on the edge of the bed and then stretching out next to me.

"Mom?"

"Ssshh. Your dad snores so when he drinks."

He must have stopped during the night, or else Mom got tired of the cramped quarters, because when I stirred later she was gone.

I awakened again at about seven. Dumb kid, I told myself. Just like you used to be, up at the crack of dawn, on Christmas Day. I rolled over, but it became very clear that I was not going to go back to sleep. Then it hit me: *Elaine's back. She's in her room, lying there, smiling.*

Knowing I was absolutely nuts, but knowing I had to *know*, I tossed back the covers and eased next door to her room. God, it looked so empty. Worse than usual, even, because Mom had cleaned it up and bought a new bed-spread. I shut the door and stood wondering if that throbbing in my head was an eggnog hangover, when I heard these strange sounds coming from the kitchen.

My first thought was, Dad didn't lock the door! Then I realized it wasn't human footsteps I was hearing, or even usual kitchen sounds. I went across the hall, swung open the louvered doors.

"Mew."

The floor was cold, but I sprawled on it, anyway, face to face with a kitten so white and

110

fluffy and adorable it looked as though it had stepped right out of a Christmas card or a calendar. It had a red ribbon around its neck, and a tag which read:

> ANDY: I'm little, but
> I'm full of love. And
> I'm all yours. XXXX

"Oh, Christie!" I said. "Oh, you're so darling!" *Christie?* Why had I called him that? Because he's a Christmas present, I told myself, as I scooped up my full-of-love kitten and nuzzled him against my neck.

I got up, and holding him with one hand, took out milk, closed the refrigerator door with my knee, and started heating a small amount in a pan. The kitten got loose, scrambled to the back of my neck, and pawed at my hair. I detached him and poured out his breakfast.

So you're the late errand Joe had last night, I thought, as I sat cross-legged on the floor, watching Christie lap at the milk. Joe really was going somewhere. It wasn't just an excuse to get Cassie out of this doom-and-gloom atmosphere.

And then another thought came to me as the cat backed away from the milk and started exploring the room. I couldn't call him Christie! What if someone—Chris—should hear of it and think, *Hmmmm . . . Chris . . . Christie!* I'd die.

111

Just die. Although my bottom was chilled from sitting on the floor, my face felt on fire. Wow, the embarrassments a person could bring on herself, all innocently!

"That settles it," I told the kitten as I scooped him up. "You're someone else, but I don't know who, just yet. We'll just have to wait and see."

"What are you going to call him?" Joe asked when finally, after brunch, we gathered in the living room. The kitten was cycloning around, pulling at ribbons, clawing tissue, and making wild dashes up a branch of the tree. A gold ball fell onto the carpet and bounced.

"Nuisance would be a good name," Dad said, rehanging the ornament.

I glanced at Mom, whose smile had no relation to the look in her eyes.

"I'll try to keep him in my room, Mom," I said. "I know you don't like cats."

"Yes, I do," she said.

Then I remembered the real reason we'd never had a cat before. Elaine had been asthmatic as a child, and the folks had thought it best not to have animal hair floating about the house. When she came back—if she came back—I really might have to keep the kitten in my room. And his name might as well be Nuisance. In public. In my mind he'd always be Christie.

I wrapped ribbons around his paws to distract him while I opened my gifts: a pink, fuzzy robe from one set of grandparents (a little on the snug side), a striped, hooded robe from the other set (there must be a message here, but I didn't get it), a tiger-eye ring, tops and sweaters, and also a V-necked navy-and-white leotard and tights set from the folks, a book about cats from Cassie, and finally, I opened the small box from Joe.

"Hey, a charm bracelet! With a gymnast figure!"

"I had a hell of a time finding it," Joe said.

"Let's see it," Mom said. I hauled myself over to her, since I intended never to take off the bracelet. "Darling," she said.

"Open your gifts, Mom," I told her. "Come on." She did, trying her best to show enthusiasm, but suddenly she put aside an unopened box and rushed from the room.

Dad, Joe and I looked at each other, then we quietly began clearing up the strewed wrappings. When we were finished, there were four groups of presents by four chairs. And under the tree lay a stack of packages. Unopened.

The next day I was in my room trying to convince Nuisance a litter box was not a toy. Mom was in the kitchen putting together some appetizers for when Rosemary stopped over later. I heard the phone ring and started for the kitchen.

"Elaine!" I heard Mom squeal.

113

I rushed up and put my head against Mom's to listen too.

"I thought I'd call," Elaine said. "Steve said I should." *Steve!* "Like he said you might be wondering about me."

"Wondering about you!" Even through her relief, Mom had to react. "We've been crazy with worry. When you didn't even call on Christmas . . ."

"Big deal, one day."

"Elaine, where are you exactly?"

"In Arizona. I told you before."

"But where in Arizona?"

"With Steve."

"How, with Steve?"

"Look, this is costing a lot of money . . ."

"Then call back collect!"

"There's nothing to say. I've told you I'm okay. What more do you want?"

"But what," Mom said in a rush, "if we need to reach you? For an emergency?"

"What could I do anyway, out here? I've gotta go now. Bye."

"Oh, Elaine . . ."

I took the silent phone from Mom's hand and crashed it onto the holder. I was so disgusted myself that I couldn't believe it when I looked at Mom and saw she was smiling. Radiantly.

"I just knew she wouldn't let Christmas go by without calling," Mom said. "I knew it."

"I guess it would have been too much of a strain on her to call on the day itself," I said.

Mom was so zonked out with joy that she didn't catch the sarcasm in my voice. "Now I have the very positive feeling that she's going to come walking through that door one of these days soon."

"What makes you think that?"

"Think? Why, she can't stay away. Not for long. She doesn't fool me one bit. She misses us. She had no other reason for calling."

Except, I thought, that Steve told her to.

"Joe," I told him later, "I really do love this bracelet." We were playing gin rummy in his room, making slow progress because the kitten kept skidding across the cards.

"From now on, every time you do something stupendous, I'll add a charm."

"Stupendous like what?"

"Graduating."

"Big whip. That's not so great."

"It will be for you. Look, dummy, you just threw away an ace." He took it and added it to his three.

"You got Elaine hoop earrings, didn't you?"

"I told you."

"And Cassie?"

Joe's hand hesitated over the pick-up pile. "A pearl on a thin gold chain." He put the card in with the others, then fanned them shut and

115

tossed them down. "Let's forget the game, okay?"

"Are you mad at me?"

"No." He picked up the kitten. His hand was as big as its head. "I think I'll go check out some friends."

"Meaning Cassie?"

Joe blew out his breath, looked at me, then said, "Cassie and I have decided to call it off. Correction. She has."

"You're not serious."

Joe set down Nuisance and stood up. "She's met someone else."

"Someone else! Who?"

Joe twisted his lips. "A guy."

I scrambled to my feet. "Meeting some other man wouldn't mean that much to Cassie. Not when she's in love with you." The look on his face tore at me, and yet I couldn't stop. "She *does* love you!"

Joe moved toward the door and turned. "That doesn't seem to be true any more. I thought you might have noticed. The gradual change . . ."

"Why did she come here Christmas Eve? Why did she, if she's going out with some other guy?"

Joe shrugged. "She still *likes* me, you know. And she's really fond of the family."

"Well, I'm not fond of *her!* So nice . . . and all the time sneaking around!"

"She wasn't sneaking. I knew she was seeing someone else, but I assumed it would fade away because I was the one special person." He shrugged. "Wrong assumption."

"But it wasn't fair of Cassie. She was your *only* girl."

"That was my idea. Andy, I really don't want to go on talking. It's not going to change anything."

"I hate her! From now on, I'll always hate her!"

"Don't." Joe's voice cracked. "Because if you do that, you'll also be hating a part of me." He left in a hurry.

Oh, Joe.

I sprawled on the floor and jumbled up the cards. You're wrong. Wrong to let love, even for a girl like Cassie, get to you this way.

And then I thought of Elaine. And Mom. Was too much love a dangerous thing?

I couldn't believe that. But there was no use trying to figure it out. Just pick up the cards and get on with the game.

I did pick up the playing cards. I stacked them in a neat little pile. And then I flung them across the room.

11

"Anyone can see you had a great time in Florida," I said to Robyn, that first day back at school. "Lucky you don't have Midlar for math. He said before the holiday that anyone who returned with a tan gets an F. Knowing him, he probably wasn't kidding."

"How are you getting along?"

"Maybe I'm becoming paranoid, but I got the feeling from a couple of looks he shot my way today that he knows about Elaine."

"Assume everyone knows."

"It doesn't seem fair that when one member of a family does something, it reflects on everyone."

"Heard any more from her?"

"No. My parents have called places that try to track down missing kids, but they just say they'll put her name on file. You don't know how I dread going home."

Robyn pulled her crocheted cap farther down over her ears and swung a muffler around her neck. It was about zero degrees outside. No one was exactly dashing out to get frostbite. "Want to come over to my house?" Robyn asked.

"I'd like to, but Mom's probably sitting alone as per usual. I'd better go cheer her up."

"Then put on a smile as you leave the building," Robyn advised. "It'll be frozen on your face by the time you get home."

We parted, and as I headed through the wind carrying powdery snow I had no thought except covering the distance home as quickly as possible. The chill cut through my jeans as though they were made of net, and my cheeks became Novocain-numb. When I stomped my feet outside the door and let myself into the house, my nose and eyes were running and I had to go to the bathroom, fast.

Later, still rubbing the shivers from my arms, I found Mom in the kitchen, running a mixer in cake batter. She made a kissing motion at me with her lips. Which was a mistake because her wrist lifted in reflex and sent chocolate globs into orbit. Mom isn't at all well coordinated. She even trips over the cord when she's vacuuming. I sometimes wonder how she ever made it as a cheerleader. Maybe some of her connections came loose when she had us kids.

"What's going on?" I asked, after she'd shut off the mixer. Something was already cooking in the oven, and the sink, from which I was wiping specks of batter, had a bunch of vegetables in it, soaking.

"Your Aunt Ellie, Uncle Herman, and Kitty are coming over for dinner."

"You're kidding. Why did you have to do a thing like that?"

"They invited us there, but we have to stick around. Just in case."

I knew Mom still felt tied to the phone, and I was sorry about that, but I blurted, "The holidays were so peaceful with them gone. Do we really have to get together with them now?"

"Yes, we do. They're very anxious to give us the news about your grandparents."

"Mom, you know that's a lot of bull. What they're really anxious to do is get the inside scoop on Elaine. That creep Kitty nearly drove me crazy during study hall with her nosy questions. I'm going to ask to get my seat changed."

Mom put her arms around me. "Honey, take it easy. It's only natural that they'd want to know."

She kissed me on the temple. Actually, I wasn't all that upset. I felt loved, and closer to Mom than I had since I'd been really little. She needed me now. Not just to keep the house going, the way she used to, but to keep her company and to keep up her spirits.

"Would you set the table for me?" Mom went back to the batter. "And put the cat in your room. He won't budge from the middle of the table. We don't need him as a centerpiece."

I glanced at Mom to see if that phrase reminded her of an old family story. Mom used to (so I was told . . . I hadn't been born yet) put Elaine in her infant seat in the middle of the table so that Joe would sit quietly, gazing at her, instead of toddling off to see if she was all right. "Our centerpiece," they called her.

Where was Elaine now, I wondered, getting out a fresh table cloth. What was she doing? And was Joe more concerned about her than he had let on? Or were most of his thoughts centered on Cassie these days?

Joe, I thought, you'll never have to worry about me. I'll be anything you want me to be. Even a good student. But I wouldn't be able to study tonight. Not with Kitty littering the place. What a perfect name for her. Kitty Litter.

The one good thing about that week was that I kept running into Chris. Not running into him, exactly, but catching glimpses of him every day in the cafeteria, now that he was no longer tied up with that stuff for the Christmas pageant. He was always, I was glad to note, in the company of boys. On Thursday (happy day!) we met, and his eyes crinkled in that smile that practically made my toes curl.

"How's it going? Your crew rolling?"

"Pretty much." (Why hadn't I washed my hair last night!)

"Next week some night after school maybe we should coordinate. Should I stop by your locker?"

I nodded, not trusting my voice.

In a burst of energy I took the sketches of the bats back to Ken Petit's house.

"No problem," Mr. Petit said. "I'll get going on the bodies. You'll have to sew on the material for the wings. What are you going to use?"

"Uh . . . black taffeta?"

"That should make a nice rippling effect when they fly. How do you make them fly?"

"Some kind of string."

"Be sure it's heavy. Maybe nylon fishing cord."

"My dad has that in the shop."

"If we put screw-eye bolts here and here," he said, marking the sketch, "it should balance them when they fly. When do you need them?"

"The play's in April."

"April?" Mr. Petit gave an aren't-you-cute kind of laugh. "Andrea, you're like your old man. Always planning ahead."

Little did he realize I was planning on impressing Chris.

I got up early every single morning the next week and washed my hair so it wouldn't get messed up during the night. Sometimes it was still damp when I went outside and little crystals froze on it. Friday Chris finally stopped by my locker.

"Oh, hi," I said, pretending surprise.

Robyn lifted an eyebrow and left.

"Gee, I have that list somewhere," I said into my locker. I could feel the blush on my face. I probably looked like a lobster. "Now, where is it?" I knew exactly where it was.

"That can wait," Chris said. "I really wanted to ask you something else. Want to go to the movies tomorrow night?"

I nearly passed out. "What for?" I said. In a *World Book of Dumb Remarks* that would have to be in the first chapter.

Chris shrugged. "We could go bowling, but the lanes are tied up with leagues Saturday."

I faked an Elaine kind of laugh. "What I really meant is, what's playing? Not that it matters. I haven't seen anything lately." I was making quite an impression.

Chris zipped up his jacket. "There's a small problem of wheels. Sometimes in this weather Dad has trouble starting the car."

123

"Maybe my dad could drive us." *Don't sound so eager, jerk!*

"Anyway, I'll give you a call some time tomorrow."

"Great." Maybe you will and maybe you won't, I thought, as he went toward the exit, shoving his hands into his jacket pockets. I wanted to rush after him and say something brilliant, something that would make him crazy to hear my voice again. Instead, I got my stuff from my locker.

It was pneumonia weather, and I was a hot candidate, crunching along, perspiring, with coat flapping open. The frigid air against my flaming face was like Noxzema on sunburn. Soothing.

I couldn't wait to get home and call Robyn. Should I? Sure, I should. She'd sensed something, or she wouldn't have buzzed off so fast. *Robyn, you've got to tell me what to say when he calls. If. And if he says their car is frozen, would that really be an excuse, a way of saying he's cooled off on the idea of taking me out?*

For a moment, when I turned the corner toward our house, I thought my watering eyes were playing tricks. Dad's car was in the driveway. In late afternoon? He's sick! He's had some kind of attack! My heart was thumping as I let myself into the house. "Dad?"

"In here, honey." He leaned around the lounger chair in the living room.

"What's the matter?"

"Nothing's the matter."

I was beside him now. "Then why . . . ?"

"Elaine's home."

"Elaine?"

"That's right." He had rather a set look on his lips.

"Where?" I looked around foolishly.

"In the bathtub." He glanced at his watch. "She's been soaking since I got home a half hour ago." He got to his feet. "Hell, enough of this." He went down the hall with me trailing along and rapped on the door, hard.

"Elaine, do you think you could drag yourself out of there?"

My sister's voice drifted lazily from the room. "In a few minutes, Dad."

"I haven't got a few minutes!"

Mom came from the kitchen. "What's the matter here?"

"Lucille," Dad said, his face darkening, "you give me this call to rush home, which I did. Only to find"—he gave the closed door a look—"to find that I'm supposed to sit waiting like some salesman. I've got work to do!"

"Just a minute." Mom left and from the kitchen said, "Rosemary, I'll call later." She came back and glared at Dad. "Are you trying to say, George, that the shop is more important than your own daughter?"

"My own daughter is taking her sweet old time so now she can wait. I'm right in the middle of inventory."

"Inventory! At a time like this?"

Dad's face got even darker. "I didn't receive an announcement of the homecoming, or I'd have rearranged my schedule."

"Hi, Mom," I said.

"Hi. George, when Elaine walked in she was so grubby-looking. And her hair . . . her beautiful hair . . . she's cut it and it was matted and . . ." Mom's eyes filled with tears. "George, she's had a terrible time. Wait until you see her."

"I'll see her all right. At dinner." Dad grabbed his coat from the living room. "Inform her that I don't want her to leave the house. And that's an order."

"All right," Mom said in a quavering voice as the front door slammed. "Oh, Andrea," she sagged against the wall and let the tears spill. "Why does he have to act like this when . . . oh, what's wrong with this family?"

"Is she really all right?"

"I hope so. But she looks so pathetic. Bone-thin, and her hair all hacked off, and her clothes. They might as well go in the garbage."

"What happened?"

"She and Steven had a falling-out, and some

friends of his drove her part way back in a pick-up truck, but then they dumped her and . . ."

The door opened and Elaine peered out. She looked like an elf in Dad's big brown terry-cloth robe. "Where is he?"

"He'll be back later. Oh, my darling!" Mom hugged Elaine to her with her face against the dripping short hair. It was quite a damp scene. "Don't ever do that to me again!"

My sister—I have to give her credit—seemed moved, but when she noticed me, she pulled away, lifted her chin, and said, "Hi, twerp."

A beat, and then we rushed into each other's arms.

"I missed you," she said. "Kind of." She smiled. Even waterlogged and bundled in that bulky robe, she had a certain class.

"What's been going on around here?"

I shrugged. "Christmas has come and gone."

"It has a way of doing that." She sneezed and wiped her nose on the sleeve of the robe. "Is there anything to eat in the house?"

"It's waiting for you in the dining room," Mom said. "Go. I'll get your slippers."

I started toward my room to dump my things.

"My God," I heard Elaine say. "There's a cat on the table!"

Dinner wasn't exactly a gala affair, although Mom had put together, for her, a terrific meal, with nothing burned. She was playing the hostess, with bright conversation, using me as her main target, since Elaine and Dad said practically nothing.

"Honey, you're not eating," Mom said for about the millionth time, frowning at Elaine's plate.

"I'm not hungry," she said, fiddling with her fork.

"She ate like a field hand a couple of hours ago," I commented.

"It's your favorite salad, too. But I guess you're tired and want to rest."

"She can rest later," Dad said. "First, we're going to have a little talk."

Elaine scowled but said nothing. I had to feel sorry for her. She looked so pale and defenseless.

"Why don't we go into the living room, where we can be comfortable?" Mom said, pushing back. "Andrea, you wouldn't mind doing the dishes, would you?"

I certainly would mind. "Can't they wait?"

From Dad's look I could tell it was no use arguing, so I began grabbing at the dishes and stacking them any old way. "I don't suppose you called Joe," I yelled, as a parting shot.

"I tried," Mom said, "but he wasn't at the dorm. Maybe you can reach him now. Tell him . . ."

"Come on, Lucille. She knows what to tell him."

"I bear glad tidings of great joy," I told Joe.

"Yeah? When did Moccasin Foot get back?"

"This afternoon. All I know is she got a ride part way and then got ditched."

"She's lucky if that's all she got."

"What do you mean?"

"What do you think I mean? Ever read the papers?"

"Uh . . . well, I guess she's all right."

"What's the temperature reading?"

"Mom—drizzly. Dad—cold but thawing."

"And how do you feel?"

"Abandoned."

"Andy, that's a temporary thing. How's the cat?"

"Getting fat."

"Just for the record, how come you called and not the folks?"

"They're in the living room, giving Elaine the third degree."

"Don't interrupt. Just tell them I'll be home one of these weekends."

"To see . . . ?" (Elaine? Cassie?)

"You."

I practically threw everything into the dishwasher, and then edged into the living room just as Dad was saying to Mom, "Are you going to tell that girl to get off the phone, or am I?"

Mom hurried off to Elaine's room.

I settled into a corner chair without attracting attention.

"If it rings again, let it ring," Dad told Elaine as she came in followed by Mom. "Now, if you don't mind," he said, "we'll get on with your story."

"There's not that much to tell," Elaine said, sitting down opposite him and scowling as per usual. "Like I told you, we hung around Tucson for a couple of days . . ."

"Doing what?"

The scowl deepened. "Making contacts."

"What kind of contacts?"

"Does it matter? Mom . . . !" Elaine gave her a look of appeal.

"Never mind *Mom*. Just answer the question."

Elaine dug what was left of her nails into the arm of the chair. "Steve wanted to set up some kind of leather craft shop with some guys he knew, but that didn't work out."

"So then?"

"So then Steve and I and some other kids went off to this place . . ."

"Where?"

"Dad, I don't know where! I didn't carry a map around with me!"

"Go on."

"It was like a farmhouse, only without any, you know, crops. We stayed around there the rest of the time, and it was really the dregs."

"What do you mean?" Mom asked.

"I mean, there was no food practically. We'd warm up a can of corn or peas, and that was it. And the house was drafty and dirty. And really depressing."

Mom made a sympathetic sound.

"One day Steve got mad at my so-called complaints and said if I didn't like it there I could head back East. I said, okay, I would. There were two guys at the house who were leaving, and they said I could come along, so we took off in their truck." Elaine blinked fast, and her voice broke a little. "I kept thinking Steve would come down the highway after me." She swallowed. "But he didn't."

Dad gave her a look that said he found all this hard to take. "You really wanted him to come after you?" he asked my sister.

"I was in love with Steve."

"After all that. You were still in love with him."

"Well, I'm not anymore!" Elaine glared at Dad, tears streaking down her face. "Is that all? Can I go?"

"Not quite." Dad shot a look at Mom, who seemed about to move toward Elaine.

"So you got into a pick-up truck with two virtual strangers . . ."

"I knew their names!"

". . . and went where?"

"Through a couple of states, and then they stopped off and stayed with some really sleazy people. When I told them I didn't like it there, they said okay, then, take off. So I did. I hitched the rest of the way home."

"What happened to the money you had?"

"I gave most of it to Steve for that—you know—shop that didn't work out."

"So you were broke when you started back?"

"Except for a couple of dollars," Elaine said.

"Why in heaven's name didn't you call?" Mom asked. "You know we'd have wired you the fare home."

Elaine shrugged. "You'd have called the police too, I'll bet. I didn't need that!"

Mom looked so desolate I went over and, kneeling on the floor beside her, rubbed one of her hands.

Dad sighed. "This whole episode sounds like something I wouldn't watch in a movie. Elaine, in my wildest dreams—"

"You don't think it turned out the way I wanted, do you?" Elaine wiped at her cheek, leaving a smear of make-up from her eyes. "I didn't plan it!"

"You never do," Dad said. "Things happen. And I'll tell you why. Because you just rush off

and do crazy things without thinking of the con-
sequences.''

"But George," Mom said, "she's safe now.
She's back. Nothing happened.''

"Something happened," Dad said. "We all
aged a little.''

Elaine gave a howl. "Now you're trying to
make me feel guilty!''

"What's wrong with that?" I piped up, leaning forward on my knees. "Why shouldn't you
feel guilty?''

Dad got up. "Guilty . . . sorry . . . I don't
know. I just hope you feel *something,* Elaine.''

Elaine glared at him for a moment. Suddenly
she twisted on the chair and began shaking with
sobs.

Mom sprang to her side and put her arms
around Elaine, as best she could. "Come on,"
she murmured. "It's all over. You're back with
us. Safe. You'd better get some rest now.''

Elaine got out of the chair and hesitated.
Then she went to Dad, put her arms around
him, and sobbed on his shoulder. He closed his
arms around her, and I thought he was going
to cry too, but he didn't.

Elaine turned back to Mom, and with arms
linked they left the room.

After they were gone, I looked at Dad, standing there like someone who'd just been robbed.
"I think she is sorry, Dad," I said.

"Maybe she is. At the moment. But I wonder . . ."

I knew what he was wondering. Would Elaine settle down now and start acting halfway human? Or would she just wait a while and go on to something else?

There was no way of knowing.

12

Mom came into the bathroom and asked if I'd mind just washing at the sink so that she could get into a hot tub. I hurried, because she was already running the water and pulling off her sweater. Mom wasn't self-conscious about being half-dressed around the family, but I didn't care for it myself.

"What's Elaine doing?" I asked, through the toothpaste.

"Trying to sleep, I guess," Mom said, scratching along her bra straps. "She's bushed."

I kissed her goodnight and went to my room. How Elaine could relax with her stereo going full volume was beyond me, but at least in that respect, things were back to normal.

I read a while, got drowsy, turned off my light, and lay there with my eyes still open. Poor Dad. Everyone else was trying to take it easy, but he'd had to go back to the shop to pick up where he'd left off this afternoon.

Elaine hadn't planned this either, but she'd come back with her Soap Opera Saga when Dad's mind should have been on the accounts. He needed more help at the office. Maybe some day Joe . . .

Nuisance jumped up on my bed and walked across my stomach.

I lifted my head. Come here, kitty, Christie . . . *Chris!* I'd forgotten about Chris and the maybe movie! I'd meant to mention it casually tonight at dinner, just to test the reaction so when Chris called . . . if he called . . .

Elaine had shot down those plans. I'd just have to blurt out the story, cold turkey, at breakfast tomorrow morning.

I was wide awake now, wondering what they'd say.

It was kind of what I expected.

"Absolutely not!" Dad looked shocked.

"Honey, you're so young. Eighth grade." Mom looked dubious.

"I just said *possibly*. You don't have to get so excited." I sloshed the milk around in my glass.

"I'm not excited," Dad said. "I'm adamant. You're not going to start dating at your age."

"They don't call it dating anymore," I said.

"What do they call it?" Mom asked with interest.

"It doesn't matter what they call it," Dad

136

said, crumpling his napkin and dropping it on the breakfast plate. "Dating, going out with boys. You're not going to do it, and that's final." He pushed away from the table.

"I'd just like to know why not." I was trying to keep a tremor out of my voice as I turned and looked Dad right in the eyes.

"You're not going to do it because I said so." He stared right back at me, then put on his sheepskin jacket and went out the back door.

Mom and I sat there, listening to Dad warming up the car and then backing out of the driveway.

"I never thought he'd act that bad," I said.

Mom started to clear the table. "Don't forget, he's upset because of inventory. And, besides, Andrea, your timing was poor, what with Elaine—"

"My timing! I didn't ask her to—"

"Please." Mom put a hand against her forehead, leaving a little grease spot. She picked up my plate. Elaine's was still there. Her Imperial Highness had not yet arisen. "My advice is, when the boy calls—"

"His name is Chris."

"When Chris calls—"

"If he calls."

Mom sighed. "Tell him . . . tell him you'll have to postpone the—whatever you call it—because a family matter has come up."

137

"I bet he'll know what."

"Then he should understand."

He'll understand I have a wacko sister, I thought, watching Mom run water over the plates. "Then what about the next time Chris calls? If he does."

"I think your dad will come around in time, Andrea. Don't push. Maybe sometime you could invite the boy—Chris—to stop by when your father's home. And then—"

"And then Dad can see for himself that Chris isn't some wild-eyed sex maniac."

"Don't talk like that. And go wake Elaine. Eleven hours of sleep should be enough."

Elaine got up willingly enough, probably because she was starving again. She ate a complete breakfast. Before, she always said the sight of eggs made her gag. The sight of *her* was not particularly appetizing. Her eyes were puffy, her hair stuck out at all angles, and her nails were pure disaster.

"Why, actually, did you hack off your raven locks?" I asked.

Elaine spooned strawberry jam onto her toast. "Head lice," she said. "All over the place." She laughed. "Don't look so grossed out. I got rid of them."

"Let's hope you did." Mom lifted a clump of Elaine's hair and zeroed in for a look. Elaine brushed Mom's hand away.

138

"You have an eleven o'clock appointment at the Style Salon to see what they can do with this mess. And then you're going to have a checkup at Doctor Gibson's."

"Mom, I'm okay."

"Then on the way home, we're going to stop off at your Aunt Ellie's."

"God! Do we have to?"

"It's either that, or they'll come trooping over here tonight."

"Go!" I said.

Elaine looked grim. "I'll go, but I'm not giving them a run-down on what happened. It's none of their business."

"Will you give me a run-down?" I asked. "I mean on some of the more interesting highlights of your trip?"

I expected an it's-none-of-your-business-either reply, but Elaine just yawned and said, "Okay, but, remember, you asked for it."

I don't know what I expected, but later when Elaine got through telling me about how no one at the farmhouse would cook or go anywhere, and about all the squabbles, I could only wonder why she'd stuck it out as long as she had. "If the scene was so rotten, why'd you stay, anyway?" I finally broke in.

Elaine paused with the emery board. (Mom wouldn't let her get a manicure at the beauty shop.) "Why? For love." She gave me a look. "You wouldn't understand."

"There are all kinds of love, you know."

Elaine unscrewed the cap of undercoat. "Oh, really? Tell me about it."

"Like love of . . . family." I waited, but she wouldn't look up. She did one hand and started on the next. "Didn't you even stop and think how everyone here felt? Mom nearly went crazy, and so did Dad."

"I didn't ask them to worry."

All kinds of things flashed through my mind. Things I could say to my sister, presenting a new image with a really sharp haircut, a slick make-up job, and a tie-around top she'd picked up on sale. I finally settled on, "You know? You're really a pain, Elaine."

She held up a hand and blew on the undercoat. "Thanks. I'll remember that. It really makes me want to stick around."

I left.

Downstairs, I got into my new gymnastics outfit and looked at myself in the full-length mirror. Was it the clothes, or was I really slimming down some? I pulled back my hair and bunched it around my face to see how I'd look with it short. No way could I ever look like Elaine.

I did limbering-up exercises on the mat and then straddled the balance beam. And that was it. The warmth and tingling sensations that usually propelled me into action just sort of drained away. Why did I feel so dragged-out?

I stood up, did a cartwheel and then a front dismount to the mat. Guilt. That's what was weighing me down. I'd had no right to tell Elaine she was a pain, even though the facts were on my side.

It really makes me want to stick around, she'd said.

What if? No, she wouldn't. She wouldn't run off again because of me. I didn't figure that prominently in her life. But what if . . . if she did? I'd never . . .

"Hey, you!"

I jumped at the sound of Elaine's voice and whirled around.

"Is that your idea of exercise? Standing in one spot? You have a phone call. Some boy." She laughed. "Don't just look at me with your mouth hanging open. Go talk to him." She watched as I walked across the room, holding my stomach in. "You know, you're getting a figure."

"Shut up," I mumbled, feeling my face flush.

"No wonder the boys are starting to call."

"A boy. And it's about the school play." I don't know why I said that.

I was relieved when Elaine went into her room and shut the door.

"Hello?" I could feel my heart thumping under my leotard.

"Hey, this is Chris. I called about tonight. There's a problem."

"There is?" I felt both relieved and let down.

"Yeah. My folks have to go someplace, and I'm stranded."

"That's all right. I—uh—it would be better for me some other time, too."

Instead of that being the end of it, Chris eased into talk about school and sports and rock groups. It was easy talking to him. The next time I wouldn't be nervous. I had the feeling there really would be a next time.

Dad became more like himself in the weeks that followed, partly because things had eased at the shop and partly because he and Mom and Elaine were all getting counseling. No one would tell me a thing about what went on at those sessions except generalities like, "We're exploring feelings."

In my own humble opinion, Elaine was getting by with murder again, running with the same old rat pack, but she did keep hours, sort of.

The fact that Elaine's disposition had improved really impressed the folks. I would have been more impressed if my sister had pitched in with work around the house.

But I wasn't about to complain. Elaine

treated me more like a human being and even started to take an interest in my looks.

"You ought to tweeze your eyebrows," she said one day.

"Why?"

"And put on some blush under your cheekbones. To slim your face."

I wouldn't let her get at me with the tweezers, but I did sit still for a make-up session.

"You have nice features," she said, "but you've got to play them up so people will notice you."

"You make it sound like looks are everything."

"Well, aren't they?"

"Some people make it on personality. Or brains."

"How nice for them. Hold still. I'm ready to do your eyes."

There was one spin-off from the counseling that worked in my favor. Dad stopped getting spastic when I mentioned Chris's name. One Saturday when I said he was going to stop by to show me how to make a chair move by itself for the play, Dad was more concerned about our pounding nails in the floor than the fact that I was having a *boy* in the house.

"What do you mean, pound nails? And what floor?"

"Just little nail holes to get the screws

143

started, and the floor in your workshop is a mess anyway, you know that."

"Just take it easy, that's all."

He left, much to my relief. I was nervous enough without having the whole family hanging around, giving Chris the evil eye.

Mom, when she met Chris, must have been pleasantly surprised, because she almost overdid the welcome. Elaine, though, barely mumbled "Hi." He could have been a paper boy or a cub scout selling raffle tickets.

Chris and I went downstairs. At the bottom step I paused, foot poised. I'd forgotten about the gymnastics equipment. What would Chris do? Would he clown around on it, as though it were a toy? Worse, would he try to get me to perform?

"That yours?" he asked, eyeing the beam.

"Yeah. I work out down here sometimes."

"Hey, great. You know Bonnie Knudsen?"

"No, but I heard she made it to the finals. You know her?"

"My brother does." He looked around. "Where's the chair?"

"Back there." Whew. That was it for the beam.

We went to the back room and set the old wooden chair in position. Following directions in the play-book, we put small screws into the floor about four inches toward the center, from each front leg.

Next, we cut two long lengths of fishing line. We stretched them out on the floor, from front to back, on each side of the chair. Then we took one of the strings and, leaving a tail in back, tied it around a back leg. We continued forward with the string and ran it at an angle through the screw eye, and then drew it back. That tag end, together with the tail end we'd left, was the right-side pull. We did the same with the left side.

"Position the four string ends in a row," Chris said, "here, back of the chair. Now pull just the two inner ones, coming back from the screw eyes."

I did. Wow! The chair moved forward.

"Now, pull the outside ones, tied to the legs."

It was like magic. The chair moved back!

"I can't believe it! It actually works!"

Chris laughed. "It has to. It's an engineering principle. Is this the chair you're going to use in the play?"

"No. Furniture has to supply one. Want to see copies of the sketches I made for the bats?"

"Sure."

I showed him the drawings. "Ken Petit's father is making the bodies and wing wires. I'll sew on the material."

"How do you make them fly?"

"It tells in the book." I showed him the page. "There are tracks, made with nylon line, and

145

then there's another line fastened to the bat. We reel them in, across stage. I'm nervous about it." What I was really nervous about at the moment was that Chris's head was so close to mine, and the dizzy feeling it gave me. I backed off. "I guess that does it. Want to go upstairs and—" I wanted to say "listen to records" but I wouldn't get my stereo until graduation—"have a Coke?"

"No, I've got things to do."

He left with a casual, "Be seeing you." Nothing about going out. Maybe his folks wouldn't let him, either. Or maybe his dad refused to chauffeur him, and Chris was too embarrassed to suggest my dad do it. Maybe he'd decided I wasn't interesting enough to spend an evening with anyway.

I called Robyn to get her opinion.

"Chris is just checking out the territory. He really likes you," she said.

"What makes you think so?" I was ready to believe anything.

"The way he looks at you."

"How does he look at me?"

"Notice next time."

"Do you think I should tweeze my eyebrows?"

"No."

That's one of the things I liked about Robyn. Direct. We talked for about an hour, and then

I went over to her house to help her decide which letters to put in the next Iris column.

Out of seventeen, five were about parents who were too strict or who boozed it up too much. Two were about teachers who sprang surprise quizzes (Midlar?) and didn't pass papers back on time. One was from a kid whose best friend was into shoplifting. Two were from kids who dealt drugs, one bragging about it. The other seven were boy-girl.

"Boring, aren't they?"

"Honestly." I leafed through near-duplicates of the I-like-him-but-does-he-like-me kind of letter I'd written and torn up.

"You'd think these kids would get their act together." Robyn sighed. "I'll use some of them, though. Gotta give the public what it wants."

I felt like a lousy Me Too. *I like him, but do a few looks and a "Be seeing you" mean he likes me?* Answer: Possibly negative.

The feelings of worthlessness I'd had at the beginning of the school year came back with double force. Who was I really? And what made me more than ordinary? The answer had to be nothing.

My grades were okay but average.

My looks were also okay but also average.

I was good in gymnastics but not good

enough to win any medals unless I got special training.

Miss Average. Miss Me Too. Miss Nobody Special. Those were the only competitions for which I could qualify.

One evening when we had an early dinner because of Elaine's counseling session, I almost asked if I could have an appointment too. But the thing was, I didn't know what I'd say if I got there. *Tell me how to be somebody special? Tell me how I fit into the scheme of things?*

The man would think I was out of my mind. No, he wouldn't. He'd listen, nod, and tell me not to worry. And I bet when I wasn't looking, he'd glance at his watch.

The weather broke suddenly in March, and one springlike weekend Joe came roaring home on his Kawasaki. It was the first time he'd seen Elaine since the Big Runaway, and they sat in her room and talked for a little while. Then, because it was Saturday night, and God forbid she should stay home, she took off with the gang.

"Doesn't she ever stick around?" Joe asked me.

I was out in the kitchen, cutting up fruit for a slush drink. "Never. This is the Hotel Marshall. A place to sleep, bathe, and refuel." I put the fruit into the blender and added milk and ice. After it was whipped into a thick mass I poured some into a glass and offered Joe a taste.

He took a swig and handed it back. "Not what I'd call the elixir of the gods. In fact, blah."

I ran my thumb along the mist on the glass, and the feeling I'd submerged upon seeing Joe came back. "Everything about my life is pretty bland," I said. "Like me."

"Hey. What do you mean by that?" One corner of Joe's lips lifted in a smile that wasn't quite a smile.

"It's true. I've got to face up to the facts, Joe. I come off as ordinary and always will."

He looked at me for a moment, then took me by the arm and sat me into a chair. He pulled up another chair so that we were face to face. "I want to tell you something, Andrea. You're not ordinary."

"Well, I'm certainly not spectacular."

"Ah, that's something else. Flashy you're not. But you know how it is with flashes. Here and then gone. That's not you. You're someone solid."

I had an impulse to pinch my waist and say, *too solid*, but instead I sat there looking at Joe.

"You're building," he said.

"Building what?"

"A firm foundation."

I couldn't help thinking of my bottom.

"In other words, Andy, you're steady."

"Boy, does that sound boring!"

"Life can't always be full of kicks. There's got to be something else going. There's a quote I came across, by Samuel Johnson. 'The future is purchased by the present.' Know what that means?"

I thought about it. "What you do every day finally adds up?"

"You've got it." He looked at me, grinned, and got up. "End of session. Pay my secretary as you leave."

"Am I leaving?"

"Sure you are, toots. I'm taking you to the flicks."

13

Life began looking up. The weather was warming. Chris began calling and stopping by the house now and then. Finally Dad relented and let me go to the movies with him, and to the indoor ice rink.

Elaine was still running around even on week-nights, but she was getting herself home earlier, and lately she'd even started criticizing some of the creeps in her crowd. I wondered if it was because of the counseling sessions, or if she was just beginning to develop some taste. But she still had her up-and-down moods.

One morning when just the two of us were at breakfast (Mom was working at Rosemary's), I suddenly realized Elaine was studying me. I blotted my mouth, but it wasn't smeary. "What's the matter?"

Elaine moistened her lips. "Remember what you said that time?"

"What?"

"That I give you a pain."

I felt uneasy.

Elaine's remarkable blue eyes shifted their look. "I'm wondering if you really meant it."

I hadn't expected this, and I didn't know how to answer.

"It doesn't matter." Elaine made little rips in the paper napkin with her fingernails. "I can't help what people think. And I can't be what other people want me to be."

"I don't want you to be any special way. All I want is for you not to hurt Mom."

"Mom!" Elaine crumpled the napkin. "Funny you should mention Mom. She really twisted the old knife the other night at therapy."

"How? What did she say?"

"It wasn't just what she said, but her whole attitude. She went on about how much it hurt her to realize I had wasted all these years— these 'golden years' I think she called them— when I could have been the most popular, the most everything . . ."

"Yeah."

"She's always been at me to be the way she used to be, 'way back when.' Well, it never has, and it's never going to happen. And if I'm a disappointment, well that's . . ." She got up and slammed her dishes into the sink. A spoon bounced and fell onto the floor.

"Elaine . . ." I'm the disappointment, I

thought, standing up. "I understand how you feel."

She whirled, anger in her eyes. "No, you don't. You couldn't possibly know how I feel. Forget I brought it up. Okay?"

"Okay."

She gave me a look and left.

I took my dishes to the sink and picked up the spoon from the floor. Maybe Elaine was right. I didn't know how she felt because that kind of pressure had never been put on me. I wasn't even in the running.

After school one day I stopped by Rosemary's shop and strolled down aisle after aisle of Easter lilies. They weren't particularly appealing to me because of their deathlike whiteness. But I did like the tulips and crocuses, even though they were artificial in the sense that they had been forced. The tulips lining our front walk were just beginning to send up shoots.

"What can I do for you?" Rosemary asked when I wandered into the back room. "Want another lesson on how to make corsages?"

"Not really. I came to see if you could still spare the artificial flowers. For batswort. For the play."

"I remember. When is it, again? I want to see it."

"The last of April. Don't expect too much.

Some of the kids still don't know their lines. Even Count Dracula. Wouldn't you think they'd be scared? I could just scream sometimes, listening to them louse up their parts."

"I know how that goes." Rosemary picked up a big bunch of lemon leaves and stuck them in a bucket of water.

"Speaking of screaming, I've been asked to do that offstage, at the opening of the play."

"How come?"

"Heidi, the girl who's supposed to, says it would ruin her voice. So Mrs. Vidal—she's the director—asked me to do it. But I don't think I can. I'm just not the screaming type."

"Then why don't you tell that Heidi to lift the sound over her regular voice, to avoid strain. Like this." Rosemary let out a scream, and I nearly fell backwards over a bunch of potted plants. It's a good thing there were no customers in the store.

We had lots of flowers around the house over Easter, thanks to Rosemary, but we didn't have Joe, thanks to the policy of his university of no long spring break but an early term ending the last of May. According to Joe, this was an advantage for students looking for summer work.

Elaine was Sulk City Revisited because Dad wouldn't give her money to go to Jamaica, where, according to her, the whole crowd was headed.

"You've already had your trip," Dad said,

154

which I honestly didn't think was the best psychology. Mom, I guess, didn't think so either, because as soon as Dad left she told Elaine she could go over to the shopping mall and load up on spring clothes.

"What about me?" I asked.

"The main thing you should be looking for is a dress for graduation. It's already late. Your Aunt Ellie mentioned that they're pretty well picked over already. "

"Graduation is almost two months away."

"But you know how it is. Stores these days get in their spring clothes right after Christmas."

The whole world was screwed up.

Elaine went off with a friend who had her own car, and I got stuck going with Aunt Ellie and Kitty.

Driving with Aunt Ellie was an experience. She gripped the wheel like one of those Indianapolis 500 drivers, while doing thirty-five an hour, and kept hitting the brake in short jerks for no reason at all.

We finally made it, white knuckles and all. Aunt Ellie said, going off to look at wallpaper patterns, "Now, Katherine, if you find a nice frock [frock!] tell the clerk to put it aside, and I'll look at it when we meet at three at the entrance of Pet World."

Robyn was sitting on one of the curved benches in the Grand Mall, waiting as planned.

Only Kitty hadn't known she was going to join us.

"How come you're here?" she asked in that wimpy voice of hers.

"Why, dear, I often come over here to observe humanity," Robyn said. "The shopping mall, a phenomenon of the seventies, should be of interest to sociologists of the future, and I may write a treatise on it. You know, the mall as recreation center for the masses, social center, playground . . ."

"We're here to shop," Kitty said, grinding out the words.

"For frocks," I said, with a sidewise glance at my cousin. "Graduation frocks."

"Graduation frocks! How nice! I'll go with you."

Kitty took off and barged into the first store, with us in pursuit. As it happened, it was Fredericks of Hollywood.

"Here's a smashing frock," Robyn said, pulling a tangerine-colored number from the rack. "Don't you love the neckline, dear?"

"It's too low and you know it. And don't call me *dear*. I'm as old as you are." Kitty clanged through a few hangers and stalked out of the store.

We went into two or three more shops, with Kitty getting more peevish by the moment. Finally she said she'd rather shop alone, and

I should be at Pet World by three if I wanted a ride home.

Robyn had found a dress in Florida over Christmas vacation, and with her help now I found and bought a dress in a soft yellow shade. We stopped for a Coke, and then I went back to meet Kitty.

"Did you find any?" I asked my cousin.

"Two possibles. What do you have in that box?"

"My dress."

"You *bought* it? How?"

"With a charge card. Why?"

"Your mother lets you . . . after . . . ?"

"After what?"

Kitty clamped her mouth shut and looked off into the distance. I knew what she was thinking. *After the way she spoiled Elaine.*

I was different. But I didn't have to explain that to Kitty or to Aunt Ellie, making her way toward us. Nevertheless, I felt guilty.

Because of conflicting activities (Count Dracula, for instance, was on the track team), we were able to rehearse only a couple of times a week. Even so, the play was slowly shaping up.

To save their voices, members of the cast just said, "Scream, scream" when they were supposed to let out blood-curdling yells. "The final week, though, you'll really have to scream,"

Mrs. Vidal said, through her usual smile. "I'd hate to have you forget the night of the play. That means you, too, at the opening offstage, Andrea." She gave me an extra special smile.

After rehearsal I got her aside, and said I didn't think I could do it.

"But why?" she said, with a pulling together of perfect eyebrows.

"It's not in me. I'm not the yelling type."

"Well, if you'd really rather not, Heidi will just have to do it. Your special effects are super, Andrea. I love those bats."

They really had turned out well. After Ken's father carved the bodies and attached wing skeletons, I spray-painted the bats black and added red eyes and white, jagged teeth. Chris, Ken, and I rigged them up and reeled them back and forth across the stage several times to be sure they worked. I must say it was pretty spectacular, the way they swooped across, with those black taffeta wings flapping in the breeze.

The final week of rehearsals before the Friday night of the play finally arrived. I was a wreck. During one rehearsal the wire slipped off the reel as Ken was cranking from his side of the stage, and the bat plopped down in the middle of the set. Once, when Dracula was supposed to disappear through a secret panel while actors held up his cape, he got stuck. Another time one of the actors tripped over the strings behind the chair and broke one, so it moved sideways instead of straight back. And on Thursday I forgot to turn on the fog machine in advance, and the mist poured out after the action.

Chris came over from the sound and light cage to show me where, in the script, I could safely turn on the machine and still not activate the mist.

"I wish I were in perfect control the way you are," I told him. His ghoulish Dracula music always came in on cue. So did the flickering lights and the sounds of dogs howling in the distance. "I'm afraid I'm going to louse up the play. I don't know why I even got involved in it."

Chris put a hand on my shoulder. "You'll know why when there's a live audience out there. It makes it all worthwhile."

I was aware of his closeness (as always) and also aware of the fact that Kitty was staring at us from the wings. She looked a little green. She hadn't a notion, when she'd whispered in study hall that Chris was cute and all the girls were after him, that he came over to our house fairly regularly now. I wasn't going to tell her, but I hoped to be around when she found out that Chris and I had gone out a few times together.

"What are you doing after the play tomorrow night?" he asked.

"I don't know. I was thinking my brother might come home, but . . ."

"Should we go out and celebrate?" He started walking with me toward the wings where Kitty was standing, and I'm pretty sure she heard, so I answered, "Sure," without bothering to add that I'd have to ask my parents. Life does have its little moments of triumph.

I was so nervous the next night I could hardly eat dinner. I was also ticked at Elaine, although I pretended it made no difference to me that she wasn't going. "Dad," I said, when he started in on her, "it doesn't matter. The play's not all that important to her."

"It's important enough for—" I got the feeling Mom kicked him under the table. "It's a big event."

"Dad," I said, "it's not as though I were onstage." If this was going to turn into a family row, I'd as soon she stay home. But Elaine, of course, had no notion of staying home. Not on a Friday night.

"It's just that Greg is moving to California, and there's a big party for him."

"Someone's always coming or going in your crowd," Dad said. "Why don't they all just clear out and get it over with?"

"Mom," I said, to change the subject, "I really love your hair. How come you got it cut?"

"They talked me into it at the shop. I hadn't planned on it. Do you think it makes me look younger?"

"Yes." I glanced at my sister, sitting there with her darkening, stubborn look. "But when Elaine cut her hair, she looked older."

"Really?" Elaine's mood brightened. Flashing a smile at Mom, she said, "You'd better not get any younger-looking or people will think we're sisters."

Mom beamed. Lately they'd had these little friendly moments.

"Mr. Moon," I said to Dad, "it looks as though you and I are the only ones who stay the same."

"Miss Moon, I would like to count on that," he said.

Nuisance jumped up on the end of the table. I scooped him off and took him along to watch me get dressed. Backstage people were supposed to wear dark, casual clothes. I knew before being picked up by my cousin and her parents, all going early, that Kitty would be wearing something new and cute. Let her. I was the one who was going to rush home afterwards, change, and go out with Chris.

Back in the dressing room it was bedlam, with the cast carrying on to crew members about how nervous they were and swearing they'd forget their lines. After they got into their costumes, they went into a room where teachers were helping everyone put on make-up and wigs. Count Dracula had to have his hair sprayed black and slicked back, and his face painted white, with spooky eye coloring.

I wanted to stick around and watch them make Kitty look old and wrinkled, but instead, I wandered onstage to check out the special effects.

"Everything's all set," Ken told me. "Don't worry about a thing. Three hours from now it will all be over."

We could hear murmurings from the audience. I wanted to peek through the curtains to see if my parents had arrived yet, but that wasn't professional.

Before long the actors began appearing. Mrs. Vidal told everyone to take places and to be quiet. Then the curtains parted, the audience quieted, Heidi screamed offstage, and the action began.

The bats flew like real-life vampires, and kids in the audience shrieked. In the second act Ken and I got the fog machine turned on on cue, and that mist really looked great, rolling in through the French doors. One of the chair strings got caught on a rough spot, but I gave it a good yank and prayed it wouldn't break. It didn't.

Chris was right. There really was a feeling of *this is all worthwhile* when an audience was out there reacting to everything we did.

162

And then the final lines, the surge of music, the applause, the curtain calls. And it was all over. I felt limp. We'd done it.

I started getting keyed up again as people began trooping onstage from the audience, shouting out congratulations.

"Leave that bat alone," I yelled at someone's little brother, who had climbed the ladder and was yanking at the cord. I retied the bat to his mooring and, while still on the ladder, looked around for my parents. The only person I saw from the family was Uncle Herman, who at that moment saw me and came over.

"Andrea," he said, "come on, I'll take you home."

"How come?" I asked, getting down. "Where are Mom and Dad?"

"They're at the house."

"Oh." They didn't waste any time hanging around, I thought. "How about Kitty?" I asked, as he took my arm and steered me through the crowd and outside.

"Your Aunt Ellie is waiting for her to get off her make-up. I'll get them later."

Uncle Herman, the one member of that family I'd always liked, was acting awfully distant. Maybe Kitty had told him I was trying to make out with Chris. I wouldn't put it past her. *Chris!*

We were already at the car, and Uncle Herman was unlocking my side.

"Could you hold it a second?" I asked. "I've got to go tell someone I'm leaving."

"Sorry, honey, we'd better go right away."

I didn't even have a chance to argue. We were in the car and moving. I glanced at Uncle Herman, who was alternately flooring it and braking. "Is something wrong?" I asked.

He glanced at me but didn't answer. And then I got it. Mom had arranged a surprise party for Kitty and me. She wanted to give me a chance to get into some other clothes before the guests arrived. Kitty, of course, would have fixed herself up before she got there.

"Uncle Herman, don't pretend. I know."

He braked so hard I almost hit the windshield.

"It's a party. A surprise party." Darn, I thought, I should have told Mom my plans. Well, at least I'd get to see Kitty's face when Chris came rolling in.

"Fasten your seat belt." He fumbled and handed me the buckle. His hand was shaking, and his face looked really strange.

I began getting scared. Something had happened. The air was full of tension.

We went a couple of more blocks and turned the corner to our street, and then I knew. There was a police car in our driveway. Elaine had run away again.

I wasn't angry. I was furious. Why did she have to do this! I hadn't made a fuss about her skipping the play, but I hadn't expected her to go out of her way to spoil it for me. If she had to run away, why did it have to be this night of all nights! And make such a big scene about it!

There were several cars parked in our driveway, behind the police car. We pulled up to the curb in front of the house.

"I'm not going in," I said, unbuckling the belt and folding my arms across my chest.

"Honey." Uncle Herman's face was white. "You'll have to face it." He got out of the car and came around and opened my door. "It won't be easy, but you'll have to face it."

His eyes had such a tense look that I got scared all over again. "She didn't get hurt, did she? Nothing happened to my sister, did it?"

Uncle Herman moistened his lips and looked away. "Your sister's all right. Come into the house, Andrea."

"I'm—I'm scared."

"Come along, Andrea. Take my hand."

My heart started doing such wild things that it seemed the only part of me that had life. I couldn't even feel my feet walking. But we had reached the front door somehow, and now Uncle Herman had his arm around me.

I saw the blurred faces of neighbors in the room, and then Dad came toward me like a big, bold figure on television.

"Did you tell her?" he asked.

"No," Uncle Herman said.

"Andrea . . . Andrea . . ." Dad's voice sounded like a wounded animal. He took hold of my shoulders, and he was shaking, and I started shaking, too, when I saw the agonized look in his eyes.

"Dad . . . ?"

"It's . . . Joe. He was . . . was coming home." Dad gave a huge shudder. "There was . . ."

"What?" I could feel myself going rigid. "There was what?"

"George, maybe you'd better . . ." someone said, touching his arm.

"There was an . . . accident, Andrea."

At that, hands took hold of Dad, and I felt someone get a grip on me.

"Leave me alone!" I twisted violently, trying to break the grip, trying not to see the frozen faces. "Where's my brother? Where is he? Dad!"

"Joe's . . ." His voice dropped. "My son is . . ."

"He's not!" I strained at the arms holding me. "HE'S NOT! DAD! TELL ME HE'S NOT!"

I broke loose and flung myself at my father, and I felt him hold me, but then there was a numbness and a blurring and a strange buzzing sound.

And the screams started . . . and screaming, screaming, screaming.

I felt myself being lifted and carried someplace and laid down, and still those screams continued. They went on and on, and figures moved around me. Then there was a sting in my arm, and through the screams everything started fading, and finally I didn't hear the screams anymore.

14

Someone was in my room, sitting on the side of the bed, when I woke up.

"Hi, honey."

I felt so strange. I could hardly open my eyes. "Mom?"

"It's me, honey. Rosemary."

It was like being in the bottom of a pool, trying to rise to the surface, only my arms were flailing through masses of goosedown, and if I didn't get out soon, I was going to be smothered.

Something cool touched my forehead, and I broke to the surface and took a deep breath.

"That's better. Here, pet, drink this."

My head was raised, and something hard touched my teeth, and then I felt something liquid. And with the first swallow, my eyes opened and memory rushed back.

"No!" I sat upright. "No. NO. NO!"

"Sssshhh, honey, lie back. Ssshhh. Shhh."

"I want Mom!"

Rosemary bit her lips. "Sugar, your mother is under sedation. Now let her rest. And you drink this, and then you rest some more too."

"Daddy . . ."

"He's . . . out. Out seeing to things. But you drink this, and then I'll go get Elaine. You want your sister, honey?"

"I want—I want—Joe! Where is he? I want Joe!"

"Baby, baby, baby," Rosemary crooned, holding me against her chest. "Cry, cry, that's all right, darling, cry," she said, rocking me back and forth. "Just let it all come out."

And I sobbed and I sobbed until my strength gave out, and I fell back on the pillow, and the down drifted back, and the hands smoothed my cheeks and let me keep breathing.

The rest of that day is like a dream, with some parts vivid, some completely forgotten, and all of it disconnected.

I remember seeing people. Relatives, neighbors, Joe's friends, strangers. Some of them—too many of them—kissed me and murmured things I didn't want to hear.

"It's all a mistake," I wanted to tell them. "There's no use your being here. Nothing has happened."

And there were scraps of talk—"motorcycle

totally demolished . . . ," "thrown clear, but . . ."—suddenly hushed when I came near.

Mom lay on the sofa all afternoon, and when I went to her, she touched my face as though I were a stranger. Her hair was all damp, and her eyes didn't quite focus.

Dad put his arm around me and led me to his room. Elaine was lying on their bed, curled up, refusing to see anyone.

"Girls," Dad said, pulling me down to the side of the bed beside him, "I think I'd better tell you what happened." He kept one arm around me and put his other on Elaine's curled-up leg.

"I don't want to hear it," Elaine said into her fists.

"He hit something in the road, loose gravel maybe, and lost control. There's not much to say, I guess, after all. It was an accident."

I burrowed against Dad's chest. "Why did it have to happen?"

"There's no use asking *why*. It happened."

"I wish it had happened to me instead."

"Don't say that, Andrea."

"Why not? It's true. I don't want to live now that he's . . ." Dad held my face so hard against him I couldn't say anything more. Or breathe. He let me go. I swallowed and took a deep breath. "I just can't believe I'll never see my brother again."

Elaine raised her head. "We will tonight, won't we, Dad? At the . . . ?"

"No. It's better to remember Joe the way he was."

That night was pure horror, with people drifting, drifting past the closed coffin . . . where Joe was.

Mom and Dad and the relatives who'd come to town stood up there, and I didn't see how they could take it, the people, the words, the embraces.

Elaine huddled in a dark corner with some friends, and I found an out-of-the-way place to sit, behind some artificial palms.

Kitty came sliding onto the folding chair beside me and would have touched me, I know, except that I pulled away from her. Kitty's face was all blotchy from crying, and I clenched my teeth to keep from saying, "What right do you have to cry?"

"Some of the kids from school were here," she said. "Did you see them?"

I shook my head no.

"Everyone feels terrible."

I turned my face a little away from her. She was making the tears start again. Why didn't she just go away!

"I guess you feel terrible too. Especially because . . . well, the reason he was coming home."

It hit me like a body blow. Horrified, I turned to face Kitty.

She shrank back from the look on my face. "It . . . no one said it," she mumbled, easing herself sideways from the chair. "But, well, if it hadn't been for your play . . ." She backed away and darted behind the palms.

Someone found me huddled there, bent over with sobs, and took me home. I don't know who.

The funeral was the next day, but I don't even want to think about that. I shut it out of my mind while it was happening. I was there, but I wouldn't acknowledge it. Mom practically passed out, I know, and I heard Elaine making a big scene, but I just stood there at the cemetery, clenching my mind, not letting anything in. I do remember holding spring flowers in my hand. Rosemary, I think, put them there. I don't know what happened to them. And once I thought I saw a face, and it started to bring back a memory, but I turned it off.

Life went on. As Elaine once said about Christmas, it has a way of doing that. But it was no kind of life at all. And it never would be again. Not without Joe.

I gave Nuisance away.

"But why?" Mom asked. She had lost a lot of weight and could have worn Elaine's clothes. "He was such a good little cat."

"He kept sitting on the table."

She gave me a long look but didn't say anything else.

Dad cut down his hours so he could spend more time with Mom. There was some talk of their taking a trip to Hawaii, but Mom made one excuse after another. "Maybe this summer . . ."

"Why don't you go now?" Elaine asked. "If you don't trust Andrea and me here alone, someone could come stay with us."

"It's not a question of trust," Mom said. "Don't ask me to leave. Just don't ask me. Not yet."

Elaine shrugged and sauntered off. Dad's eyes and mine met. We knew why Mom wouldn't leave. She went out to see . . . to the place where Joe was . . . every day.

The teachers at school didn't lean over backwards being kind, and I really appreciated it. Sympathy, sometimes, is harder to take than indifference.

With the kids it was something else. At first they all crowded around, saying how terrible it was, and how could I stand it, but the cold look on my face soon put a stop to that. Then they took just the opposite approach, trying to draw me into stupid conversations about school events, and I mumbled out answers that didn't say much. I could tell they were relieved when I walked away.

I even avoided Chris. He got the message after a while and kept his distance.

One Saturday morning in May I got a call from Cassie. "Andrea, I'd like to take you to lunch," she said. "Could I? Today?"

It was habit, now, not to let myself feel anything. Not even surprise. "Okay," I said, without interest.

She picked me up and took me to a quiet little restaurant that looked like an indoor garden.

"I've missed you," she said. "I've wondered how you were."

The bar waiter took our order for a Coke and something for Cassie with a twist of lemon.

"Anything interesting going on at school?" she asked.

"Not really." I talked a little about our basketball team winning the state finals, but it was the kind of conversation that didn't go anywhere.

"Are you excited about graduation?" Cassie asked, after a silence.

"No."

The waiter brought our drinks, and relief showed on Cassie's face. "Well," she said, lifting her glass toward me, smiling. The smile faded, and her hand hesitated in midair.

"Cheers," I heard myself saying.

Her look was like a silent *thank you*.

Things eased up a little after that. We ordered, and during the meal Cassie talked about flying. She had transferred to overseas flights and had some fairly interesting stories to tell. But then, when we were finished, Cassie seemed uneasy again. She glanced toward the bill, lying face down on the tray, but didn't turn it over.

I guessed what had happened. Cassie had changed purses and forgot her wallet. Mom was always doing that. I tried to remember how much I had on me. A couple of bills and some change.

"Andrea . . ."

"Ummm?"

She picked up her bag and snapped open the clasp. She took out a tiny white box. "I've been holding onto this for a long time, waiting, trying to work up the courage . . ."

I stared at the box.

"I actually had it with me the day of . . . out there . . . thinking maybe if I gave it to you it would help. But when I saw you holding those flowers and looking . . ." Cassie glanced down, and when she looked up again, the lower lashes stuck to her cheeks. "I couldn't, then. It wasn't the right time at all."

She took my hand, put the box into it, and closed my fingers around it. "So now, here it is."

"What is it?" My hand started to tremble.

"Something from Joe. Oh, please, don't cry."

I dropped the box and put my hand to my mouth. "How can it be from Joe?" I started shaking.

"He bought it before Christmas and asked me to keep it for him, until your graduation. That was before I told him . . ."

"That you didn't love him anymore?" I said, through my fingers.

"Those weren't my words, Andrea. Joe and I had a lot going for us, but I . . . I sensed it wasn't going to work out. I've felt terrible, really awful about what happened. But I won't feel responsible."

"There's no reason why you should. It was my fault!" I shoved away from the table and rushed around carpeted corners until I found a door labeled Ladies.

Cassie came right after me and knelt in front of me as I rocked back and forth on a bench, shaking with sobs.

"Hey, what is this *fault* business?" Cassie pulled my hands from my face and held them against my chest to make me stop rocking. "Look at me, Andrea. What is this you're saying?"

"It was my fault he came home. And got killed." Crying and hiccupping, I told her about

176

the play, and how he'd wanted to surprise me. "If I hadn't made such a big deal about that rotten, stupid play, Joe would still be alive," I finished, lowering my head.

"Now you stop that! You simply stop that!"

I raised my head, shocked by her tone.

"I am not going to let you talk like that or think like that and ruin the memory of everything good between you and your brother."

"But he—"

"He tried to come home because he loved you. And he cared. And an accident happened. That accident had nothing to do with you. And if you go on hurting yourself and shutting everyone out, you're not the kind of girl Joe believed you to be."

I swallowed. "What did he believe me to be?"

"Someone strong. Someone special. Steady. A girl who knows what is worthwhile and how to keep her balance. No matter what." She handed me a Kleenex. "Now, mop up," she said.

She stood by while I splashed cold water on my face, and then with a concerned, "Okay, now?" she left me to blot my face with paper towels while she went out to pay the bill.

At home, as I was getting out of the car, she handed me the box again. "He wanted you to have this," she said. "Don't deny him."

I took it and then leaned over the seat and kissed her. "Thank you, Cassie." *For loving Joe*, I thought. *For bringing him back to me*. "For lunch," I said.

"For lunch," she whispered against my cheek. "I thank you too, *Joe's Andrea*."

15

Things started getting better after that. I don't mean to say that my world suddenly turned up stardust and sunshine. There were still times when the thought *Joe's dead* would strike me like a blow on the chest by a volleyball. And often at night I wouldn't want to go to sleep because sleep made me forget, and waking up made me remember with a fresh, stabbing pain. I watched a lot of late-night movies.

School got easier to bear because the kids actually did forget, or else they were caught up in other things. I knew I'd stopped being a curiosity the day Midlar jumped on me about a late assignment, and no one looked shocked.

One day the kid I'd given Nuisance to asked if I wanted him back.

"How come?"

"We can't get him to stop sitting on the table."

"You can't? That's very strange."

So Nuisance came home and, with a bow around his neck, became our centerpiece once again. "Isn't it funny," Elaine said, "I've outgrown my allergy."

Mom stopped working at Rosemary's because she said she couldn't stand the smell of masses of flowers. She tried going out to lectures and luncheons and things with women friends, and doing a bit of volunteer work, but she was no good at it. Forgetting, I mean.

"As soon as school is out, we're going to take a trip," Dad said. "Somewhere."

"I'm not going," Elaine said. "I'd miss out on too many things if I left."

"Now, just a minute . . ."

"Dad, why don't you let her stay if she wants to?" I heard myself saying.

Elaine sat there twisting her now shoulder-length hair. I walked over to her and touched it. I felt sorry that my sister had never allowed herself to be close to Joe or to anyone. Digging roots, all alone, was a hard thing to do.

Elaine brushed my hand away. "Maybe I will go," she said, "if it's somewhere good." Her look softened as she glanced at Mom.

As for Chris, he and I got back together again. I don't know how it happened. We just did.

"What are you doing graduation night?" he asked one evening.

180

"My Aunt Ellie's having a little get-together. Want to come?"

"If it's all right."

"I'm sure it will be. But I'll ask. Robyn will be there too, for a while."

Alone in the house on the afternoon of graduation, I sat cross-legged on my bed and thought about the things that had happened since school began . . . the fun times, the hard times, and then—no, I wouldn't think about that.

My whole school year up until that final event (which I wouldn't think about) had been colored by Elaine and her behavior. I would never let her affect me like that again.

My sister was still shooting off in all directions, slapping away at hands that tried to help. But not as much as before. She still let her stereo blast and was as sloppy as ever in her room, but in some ways she seemed to be getting, as they say, more mellow. Like last night, she suddenly came into my room and said to me, "I'll take the camera to your graduation. You'll want pictures, I guess."

I started to say: *No. Joe once promised he wouldn't, because I'd be embarrassed.* But I didn't want to turn off what was, for Elaine, a really big concession. "Thanks," I said. "I'll do the same for you next year."

"Next year." She scooped Nuisance off my

bed and, sitting, held him against her cheek. "Sometimes I wonder if I'll ever make it."

"Why wouldn't you?" I asked, uneasily.

"My track record, you've got to admit, isn't all that great."

"But you'll have enough credits to graduate, won't you?"

"If I stick with it, yes."

Then do it, I almost said, but I didn't want to sound like one of those positive-thinker types. "They say senior year's the best." I'd heard that somewhere, maybe from Mom.

"Sure, it's great if you've got a lot of friends. But most of mine won't be around."

The drop-outs. The goof-offs.

"So can't you make new friends?"

Elaine stood Nuisance on his hind legs like a rabbit, and crossed his front paws. "You don't know the way kids are in high school. Cliques. You're in or you're out. And I'm . . ." She got up and handed the cat to me. "Oh, forget it. I didn't mean to come off as a pain again."

"Elaine! When I said that, I didn't really—"

"Sure you did." She shrugged. "Why not? You just said what everyone else was thinking. Mom, Dad, even Joe."

"Joe loved you!"

"I know that. It just cracks me up, though, sometimes, to think . . ."

"What?"

"That I never once called him or even hung around when he was home."

"Don't, Elaine."

"All right." She gave that same kind of crooked smile I used to see on my brother. "I guess he understood. He was that sort of guy." She left the room, but once again Joe was back.

Now, sitting cross-legged on my bed, the day of graduation, I knew it was no use trying not to think of Joe. He was always hovering in my mind, helping me keep my balance, steadying me when I wavered. Just as he'd steadied me on the balancing beam when I was little. Suddenly, with guilt, I remembered that he'd left behind a reminder of how close we'd always been. And what had I done? Snatched it from my wrist and shoved it out of sight when he'd deserted me.

Slowly I got up from the bed and went to the desk, and reaching back into the drawer, retrieved the chain. My fingers touched something else—the little white box Cassie had handed me, and which I'd never opened.

Trembling, I untied the ribbon now, and opened the box. Inside on a square of cotton lay another charm for my bracelet, a tiny silver graduation cap.

It hit me. It hit me so hard I almost crumbled. But I stood there and fought the tears and the

183

thoughts that could do me in for the day. I just couldn't let myself collapse.

With the scissors from my manicure set I opened the tiny link and fastened the graduation cap next to the gymnast figure on my charm bracelet. I put it on my wrist. And then blinking against the mist in my eyes, I went down to my basement room.

Balanced on the beam, one foot in front of the other, arms outstretched, I said, "Look at me, Joe."

"Touch me now and then," he used to say. *"Touch me if you need to."*

I would never lose the need to touch him now and then. But letting go was part of moving on. It was time to trust my own sense of balance.

Step by step, move by move, I'd make it. I was someone strong. Someone special. Steady. Maybe even the girl Joe believed me to be.

Elaine's voice called down the stairs. "I met someone at the door with a package for you. Flowers."

"Who from?"

"How should I know?"

I did a forward dismount and raced up the stairs.

"You look a mess," Elaine said, handing me the box.

"Thanks."

"Well?" she said, as I hesitated.

184

Inside, nestled in stiff green tissue was a pale yellow rose. I knew who'd sent it, because he'd asked the color of my dress.

"Who's it from?" Elaine asked. My sister had never ever received flowers from a boy.

"It came from Rosemary's shop," I said. And then I thought, Now I'm protecting her, the way Mom has always done. "It's from Chris."

"Mmmmm. It's a good thing he can't see you now."

"I'll look okay tonight."

Elaine took the rose, sniffed it, and handed it back. "Not terribly original but not bad for beginners."

Her look lingered on me a moment, and then she left, went to her room, and closed the door. In the sudden stillness I thought, Elaine, I hope your future will be strewn with flowers.

How or when that could happen I didn't know. It was something my sister would have to work out for herself.

About the Author

STELLA PEVSNER was born in Lincoln, Illinois, and attended Illinois State University and studied advertising at Northwestern. She and her husband live in a suburb of Chicago with a multitude of cats. They have four grown children, all confirmed animal lovers. Ms. Pevsner is the author of *AND YOU GIVE ME A PAIN, ELAINE* and *CUTE IS A FOUR-LETTER WORD*, available from Archway Paperbacks, and the Minstrel Book *ME, MY GOAT, AND MY SISTER'S WEDDING*.